"All right," he conceded.

"All right, what?" she asked warily.

"All right, you can do it," he told her sternly, "but you have to promise me one thing."

She leaned forward in her seat, her eyes now sparkling with excitement. "Anything."

"You have to promise that if it gets to be too much for you, you'll tell me."

"I promise," she told him readily.

He stared at her grimly, wondering if he had just lost his mind. He reached forward, extending a curled pinkie finger. She lifted surprised eyes to his, and then stared at his finger as though it were a rattlesnake about to strike. It had always been their most solemn vow, and he knew that once given, she would never break it.

Her face was wreathed in indecision. Finally sighing in capitulation, she reached forward and joined her curled pinkie with his.

"Pinkie promise," she agreed reluctantly.

Satisfied, he leaned back and studied her frowning face. "Now, what do we do about your folks?"

Books by Darlene Mindrup

Love Inspired Heartsong Presents

There's Always Tomorrow
Love's Pardon
Beloved Protector
The Rancher Next Door
Stagecoach Bride

DARLENE MINDRUP

is a part-time secretary, part-time author and full-time wife. She lives in Arizona where the sun is hot and the food is hotter. Having a passion for history, she has taken that passion and turned it into stories that she hopes will make that history come alive for her readers. Her children are grown and gone from home, but still the joy of her heart. When she is not working or writing, she loves quilting, cross-stitch, reading and working with the Linus Project.

DARLENE MINDRUP

Stagecoach Bride

HEARTSONG
PRESENTS

Recycling programs
for this product may
not exist in your area.

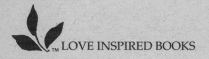 LOVE INSPIRED BOOKS

ISBN-13: 978-0-373-48728-8

Stagecoach Bride

Copyright © 2014 by Darlene Mindrup

www.Harlequin.com

Printed in U.S.A.

For the Lord does not see as man sees,
for man looks at the outward appearance,
but the Lord looks at the heart.
—*1 Samuel* 16:7

To Aurora, Grandma's newest little angel

Chapter 1

February 1859

"I'm telling you for the last time, I can't use no woman driver."

Amanda Ross stared at Mr. Dailey, the Butterfield agent, in frustration, and then glared at Adam Clark's buckskin-clad figure leaning against the office's pine-slatted wall. Adam grinned at her. She had hoped upon hope she would see him when she initiated her scheme to come to Memphis. However, if he had just waited a few moments longer to enter the office, she wouldn't be having this conversation.

Cold Memphis early-morning sunshine beamed through the open doorway and slanted across the agent's heavy wooden desk. Amanda moved into it as she leaned forward—the better to impress the little roly-poly man seated behind it. This was her big chance to prove to her family she wasn't a fragile china doll that would break at the least amount of pressure. She had to get this job!

"Then if I can't be the driver, how about the conductor?" she argued.

Mr. Dailey's incredulous eyes squinted under beetling brows as he appraised her: abundant brown tresses hidden by a small hat, a Remington revolver strapped to her hip behind buckskin jacket and breeches, and small feet clad in buckskin moccasins. Regardless of the fact she could easily have been mistaken for a man dressed as she was, Amanda still stood little more than five feet tall. It was clear Mr. Dailey held the same reservations about her abilities that made her family so overprotective of her.

"Conductor my foot. I don't need no woman on my stage line, especially in such a responsible position."

Amanda placed her hands on her hips and glared at the man. She had expected some measure of resistance, but the agent had dug in his heels harder than a mule fighting the halter. The ticking of the pendulum clock on the wall sounded overly loud in the tense silence following his statement.

"Now, look here, Mr. Dailey. If the Good Lord thought enough of a woman to entrust her with His most prized possession, His only begotten son, then perhaps you should give a little more consideration to that same fairer sex."

Mr. Dailey's teeth snapped together in aggravation, his lips thinning to a hard line. "Don't you dare go preachin' to me," he told her curtly.

Amanda fixed her pleading gaze across the room on Adam, hoping for support. He had come into the office just as she was about to convince Mr. Dailey to take her on as a driver for the Butterfield Overland Mail line, which ran from Missouri all the way to San Francisco. The infrequent letters she had received from Adam about his job as a driver for the stage line had given her the idea in the first place.

Adam had stopped in the doorway as though he'd been

shot, his hazel eyes widening at the sight of her. Although she hadn't seen him in several years, and even though she had changed her appearance, he had instantly recognized her. Her face had burned at his appalled look. Mr. Dailey had been shocked and then angry when Adam had inserted his nose into her business and informed him in no uncertain terms that Amanda was not a he, but a she.

One look at the agent's furious face and Amanda had seen her chance of becoming a driver sliding down the proverbial drain. The fact that it was obvious from his cherry-red complexion that he was embarrassed to have been fooled by her costume didn't help matters, either.

She glanced at Adam again in frustration. She and Adam had known each other since she was a babe. He was a close friend of her family, and she knew she had no hope of avoiding the interrogation—not to mention the chastisement—that was certain to come. In the meantime, he simply watched her argue with the agent, a supercilious look on his face. No doubt he would tell her father where she was and what she was trying to do. Her father would haul her back to Nashville and lock her in her room until she agreed to his Machiavellian idea of a marriage arrangement. She cringed at the thought.

Adam shifted against the wall, arms crossed over his chest, the buckskin fringe on his shirt moving when he shrugged his broad shoulders at her pleading look. One dark eyebrow lifted at her challenging glare. He pushed back his hat with one finger, revealing the dark hair beneath. His white-toothed grin made it perfectly clear he would do nothing to help.

She scowled, and his lips twitched, amusement causing his hazel eyes to shift from brown to green, the way they always did when he found something humorous.

Fixing Mr. Dailey with the most imperious glare she could muster, she motioned toward Adam.

"You can ask Adam. He knows me. He knows I can ride as good as any man. I can even outshoot him."

Out of the corner of her eye, she could see Adam tense, the amusement of just seconds ago gone from his expression and replaced with a cautionary frown. His chiseled features and the angled planes of his face became at once almost unrecognizable. The laughing young boy of her youth had become a hardened man with secrets in his eyes. She studied him, trying to see the boy she remembered so well, until Mr. Dailey sighed, his patience clearly at an end.

"I don't care if you can outshoot, out-rope, out-anything! The answer is no."

The sound of a steamboat's whistle as the boat cruised up the Mississippi River nearby interrupted the ensuing silence. Before she could gather her thoughts to argue further, a male voice checked their conversation.

"If I might interrupt a moment."

Mr. Dailey turned with fawning attention to the impeccably dressed dandy who had followed Amanda in the door earlier.

"Yes, sir?" Mr. Dailey said, ignoring Amanda's huffing protest at her instant dismissal. "How can I help you?"

He stepped forward. "Perhaps I can be of assistance to the…" He hesitated, a frown wrinkling his face with distaste a moment before it morphed into an appealing smile. "The young lady."

Amanda studied her unexpected champion. Slightly taller than Adam, he was an impressive man. He had enough good looks, with that black hair and those vivid blue eyes, to set most female hearts to thrumming, and although his British accent might be off-putting to some, she found it rather intriguing, despite his finding her attire distasteful. At least, she assumed his aversion to her was because of her unconventional clothing.

On the other hand, his clothing was the finest she had

ever seen, and she'd bet her bottom dollar his tie pin was pure gold.

He tugged at his gold cuff links, straightening his sleeves before fixing a condescending look on Mr. Dailey.

"If you would consider allowing Miss…?"

Those vivid blue eyes settled on Amanda with a powerful impact, and she had to untwist her tongue before she could answer him. "Uh…Ross. Amanda Ross."

His eyes carefully blank, he turned back to Mr. Dailey. "As I was saying, if you would allow Miss Ross to accompany the stage, I will pay her fare."

"Now, wait just a minute!" Adam pushed off the wall, his face as dark as a thundercloud.

The Brit glanced at him, lifting one disdainful brow in inquiry as to Adam's reason for interfering in something that didn't involve him. Unconcerned blue eyes stared into narrowed hazel ones, which had suddenly turned almost black in anger. The men reminded Amanda of two cock roosters challenging each other over disputed territory. She had never seen Adam so ruffled.

She swallowed hard at the cold look on his face. Nostrils flaring, teeth gritting, he was one step away from doing something that surely wouldn't be good for any of them. The other man would do well to back away from that intimidating look. Adam rarely bluffed and, even though the other man was taller, with Adam's firmly muscled body, she had no doubt who would turn out the victor.

Thankfully, Mr. Dailey interrupted their silent exchange.

"I'm sorry, Mr.…?"

"Nightington."

Mr. Dailey nodded, casting a wary eye Adam's way. "Mr. Nightington. Did you say you were willing to pay Miss Ross's fare?"

Rustling from the corner of the office near the Franklin stove drew their attention, and a woman stepped from the shadows into view. Her wool dress whispered softly against the wood floor and, as she moved into the sunlight, Amanda's mouth literally dropped open.

She was the most beautiful woman Amanda had ever seen. Her golden hair crowned a perfectly flawless oval face. Her blue eyes twinkled in amusement as she noted Amanda's hanging jaw, quietly accepting the admiration she must surely receive wherever she went. Rose-red lips nearly matching the color of her dress curved in a smile, exposing perfectly even white teeth. She inspected each person in the room, her eyes lingering just a moment longer than necessary on Adam. Her rose fragrance drifted about her in a scented cloud as she approached.

She was dressed in the height of high fashion, but Amanda didn't envy the woman her attire despite the chill February temperatures. Too often she herself had been forced by propriety to wear the layer upon layer of clothing deemed necessary by high society, but which restricted movement—so much so that it left room for nothing except sitting around and looking pretty. Amanda's buckskin outfit was more to her taste and much more comfortable. So why did she suddenly feel dowdy in comparison?

"If I might explain," the woman suggested, her British accent more melodious than Mr. Nightington's. Her eyes fixed with confident interest on Adam. "What my brother is trying to say is that we have to get to San Francisco on Thursday's stage, and he is reluctant to allow me to travel in the presence of so many men without a female chaperone."

"Now, wait just a minute," Amanda interrupted angrily. "If I wanted to buy a fare, I am perfectly capable of purchasing my own. I am no one's chaperone! I came here to drive, and that's exactly what I intend to do."

"Conduct," Mr. Dailey disagreed before realizing what

he had said. Snapping his lips together, beetling brows drawing into a frown, he waved his hands furiously. "That's not what I meant!"

"Besides," Adam told the blonde beauty, his appreciative look sliding over her slowly and setting Amanda's teeth on edge. "Even if Dailey here allowed Amanda to drive, the drivers only travel for sixty miles and conductors one hundred and twenty. There are new drivers and conductors all along the route. That would leave you without a chaperone for the rest of the 2641 miles. What will you do then?"

Mr. Nightington glared at Adam as though he was about to do him a physical injury, his hands fisting at his sides. "I said I would pay her fare as a passenger. I had no intention of implying that she would be either a driver or a conductor, whatever that is."

His sister placed a restraining hand on his arm and gave them each a cool smile that brought a swift frown to Amanda's face. Warning bells went off in the back of her mind, though she wasn't certain of their cause. Her instant antipathy toward the woman was not a common occurrence in her experience.

"If I might begin at the beginning," Miss Nightington said, and it seemed to Amanda the other woman had to forcibly drag her gaze from Adam to focus on Mr. Dailey. Amanda couldn't blame her because, next to her brother's dapper appearance, Adam stood like a towering testament of unadulterated manhood without even trying.

"My name is Rose Nightington, and this is my brother, Evan. We need to get to San Francisco before the end of next month. It's imperative."

She blinked her long, dark lashes at Mr. Dailey, flashing him a pearly smile. His eyes widened, his Adam's apple bobbing as he swallowed hard. Tugging at his bow tie, he cleared his throat and told her, "Well, I'm sure that can be arranged. But as for a chaperone…"

Evan impatiently pulled his wallet from his inside coat pocket. "How much?"

Mr. Dailey glared at him. "You don't understand."

"I understand perfectly," he disagreed coolly. "How much will it take to make this happen?"

Amanda felt as though matters pertaining to her own life were suddenly being taken from her hands. She was about to speak up when she glanced at Adam and saw his eyes were fixed intently on Evan Nightington. The tick in the corner of Adam's cheek warned her he was rapidly approaching the end of his patience, and from past experience, she knew that wasn't a good thing.

When Evan started counting out hundred-dollar bills, Amanda's mouth once again about hit the floor. Although she came from a wealthy family, she had never seen someone flaunt money so boldly.

"Mister, I'd be careful if I were you," she told him, warily glancing around to see how many people were privy to their conversation. There was only one other man in the room, and he seemed more interested in the stage timetable on the wall.

Evan's sister threw him an icy glare. "I agree. Put that away."

She turned to Amanda, her perfect smile crawling over Amanda like a slithering snake. She shivered, and doubted it came from the near-freezing temperatures. The woman put her distinctly on edge. Perhaps it was because Rose had barely taken her eyes off Adam, though why that should concern Amanda, she had no idea. He was big enough and old enough to take care of himself.

"Miss Ross, I… We would make it worth your while if you would consent to accompany me as a chaperone."

Amanda wanted to let the woman know in no uncertain

terms that she wasn't interested in her money. Perhaps if she didn't already have enough of her own, she might be tempted, but her desire was not for money, but a chance to show what she was capable of.

She glanced at Adam again and noted the imperceptible negative shake of his head. She then looked at Mr. Dailey, who blinked at her with owl-like eyes awaiting her decision.

She drew herself up to her full height, which she knew wouldn't impress anybody, and shook her head. She saw Adam close his eyes, puffing out a slow breath of relief.

"I want to drive or conduct," she told them all, and Adam's lids flew back open. His lips pressed tightly together, his hazel eyes holding a warning she prudently ignored. Mr. Dailey was already shaking his head.

"It ain't gonna happen."

"Mr. Dailey," Evan argued, "I happen to know that the Butterfield is seriously in debt."

Amanda blinked in surprise at this bit of information, and saw Mr. Dailey wince, giving credence to the statement. So it was true! How on earth could Evan Nightington be privy to *that* kind of knowledge? Her suspicions of the brother and sister were growing by the minute, and the look on Adam's face verified she wasn't the only one with reservations about them.

"If we can manage to work this out somehow, I will pay you ten thousand dollars."

Mr. Dailey's eyes nearly popped from his head, his bushy mustache twitching up and down in nervousness. He cleared his throat twice before he could finally speak.

"What you need, Mr. Nightington, is a private service. I suggest you consider checking in at the shipping office."

Brusquely pushing Amanda aside, Evan took her place and leaned across the desk to glare into the other man's eyes.

"I haven't time to take a ship. I already told you that."

He straightened slowly, his intense eyes staring mesmerizingly into Mr. Dailey's. He lifted a dark brow enticingly. "Ten thousand dollars, Mr. Dailey. What do you say?"

Rose Nightington pressed her lips tightly together, glaring at her brother's back. Her delicate nostrils flared as she sucked in a breath to obviously hold back words Amanda felt fairly certain no lady would ever utter. It would seem she was not in complete agreement with her brother, yet she said nothing. That was certainly curious—Rose Nightington seemed much more a force to be reckoned with than her sibling.

Amanda looked at the superintendent, waiting for him to tell Mr. Nightington what he could do with his money. Instead, Mr. Dailey chewed nervously on his bottom lip, glancing at the instructions to Butterfield employees posted on the wall. Amanda followed his look, and a portion at the bottom of the page jumped out at her.

"It is expected of every employee that he will further the interests of the Company by every means in his power...."

There was hesitation in Mr. Dailey's voice when he spoke. "Even if I did let her drive, there's still the matter of there being only sixty miles."

Amanda's heart took an excited dive and then just as quickly soared. He was actually considering it!

Thank You, Lord! Thank You! Thank You! Thank You!

Adam stepped forward, eyes blazing with enough anger to curl the agent's bushy mustache. "You're not serious!"

Evan turned and fixed his narrow eyes belligerently on Adam. "Why don't you mind your own business?"

When Adam's hands flexed, Amanda knew it was time to intervene.

"Adam, please." There was more to those two pleading words than anyone else in the room would comprehend, but Adam understood what she was intimating.

He glared at her, his posture rigid. "Absolutely not!"

* * *

Without saying another word, Amanda continued to plead with those incredibly violet eyes. Adam sighed inwardly. Amanda might not be much to look at otherwise, but he had never been able to hold firm when she turned her soulful orbs on him. And time after time, he had acceded to her will. But this? No, *this* time, he would stand his ground. This was not some little childhood prank she was talking about. She could be killed!

"No, Amanda," he reiterated, and her shoulders stiffened, her eyes darkening to a near-plum color in anger. He sighed again. He knew that stubborn stance. He glared back at her with a look that matched her own, and then trumped it. If he had to hogtie her and take her back to Nashville, that's just what he would do.

Evan Nightington turned back to Mr. Dailey, disregarding Adam's baleful look, which he would have taken heed of if he'd been wise.

"Perhaps I could hire the entire stage for ten thousand dollars."

What was so confounded important that the man would throw away money like that? Somehow, Adam didn't think it could be anything legitimate, which only made him more determined than ever to put a stop to Amanda's foolishness.

Mr. Dailey rubbed his jaw in thought as he continued to study the Englishman. Probably, like Adam, wondering if he really had that kind of money to throw around. Apparently, the thought was making the man reconsider his standpoint on women drivers. His skeptical gaze focused on Adam.

"Is Miss Ross really able to handle such a job?"

Adam opened his mouth to disavow any such claim but, truth to tell, he couldn't. There wasn't a doubt in his mind that Amanda could not only handle a team of horses, but probably do it in such a way that she would outdo other Butterfield drivers in the process.

And as for conducting, well, anyone who could manage an estate the size of Amanda's father's could easily handle such a task. She might be tiny, but a powerful lot of talent was packed into that pint-size package.

He remembered a time when she was fifteen years old and she had been in a wagon with the foreman of her father's plantation when he had suddenly had a heart attack, keeled over and dropped the reins. Feeling the release, the horses had panicked and took off. Amanda had stopped the runaway wagon by jumping onto its tongue and grabbing the bridles of the horses to pull them to a stop. Could she handle a stage?

"She could do it, yes, but…"

"Well, then." Evan aimed a smile full of charm at Amanda. "If you are certain this is what you would like to do?"

Adam gritted his teeth. The Englishman made it seem as though he were bestowing some great favor on Amanda. He had to give the guy credit for knowing just the right thing to say. No one had as much determination as Amanda when she had made up her mind to do something, especially when someone doubted her. It would be easier to hold back the rushing tide of the ocean.

Adam interrupted before Amanda could do something foolish, like agree to this harebrained scheme.

"No one, and I repeat, no one, can drive twenty-eight hundred miles at one time without stopping except to change horses."

Mr. Dailey turned startled eyes to Adam and stared at him for several long seconds, blinking hastily as though just coming back to reality. He shook his head slightly, shoulders drooping, and sighed.

"Mr. Clark is right," the agent said. "That's just not possible. And the Butterfield line is, after all, a mail coach. No matter what, the mail must get through on time."

"It would be possible if two people co-drove," Amanda argued. "If one driver rested, while the other driver drove."

Mr. Dailey was already shaking his head. "There is a reason our drivers only drive particular stretches of road. They know those roads like the back of their hands because they often have to drive at night in total darkness." He shook his head regretfully, seeing ten thousand dollars flying out the window.

Rose Nightington spoke up again, her melodious voice somehow soothing in an environment grown tense with hot tempers. She studied Amanda several seconds, her doubt about allowing Amanda to control a stage and six large horses reflected in her face.

"Perhaps if Miss Ross conducted, she would be able to sleep while the driver drove."

Amanda nodded vigorously. "That's a great idea. That would work. Don't you think so, Mr. Dailey?"

Adam wanted to reach out and pound something. He couldn't believe Mr. Dailey was actually considering it. Had the whole room gone absolutely insane? The idea was so ludicrous, he couldn't believe the Nightingtons had asked it in the first place, and it was beyond amazing that Mr. Dailey was stewing the proposition over.

"No!" Adam objected again, a tad more heartily this time. "Amanda is not taking a twenty-eight-hundred-mile trip!"

"And exactly who are you to speak for Miss Ross?" Evan snapped, his blue eyes glowing with anger and frustration. Adam was fairly certain the man's money had always cleared any path he chose to take. He undoubtedly didn't like being thwarted.

"Yes, Adam," Amanda almost purred, her eyes sparking dangerously. "Who are you to tell me what I can and can't do?"

So she thought she had gotten her way, did she? Well, she could think again.

"I'm the one who is going to march over to the telegraph office and contact your father, that's who."

The color leached from Amanda's face in shocked surprise. "You wouldn't!"

He folded his arms across his chest, feet planted apart. They glared at each other for several seconds, neither willing to give an inch.

"If Mr. Clark is so concerned for Miss Ross's welfare," Rose inserted quietly, "perhaps he would like to come along."

Adam looked at her, really looked, for the first time. She was something to behold with all that gold hair and those ruby-red lips. He had never seen someone with her kind of flawless beauty outside the theater. But the coldness in her icy-blue eyes ruined the picture.

The look she gave him in return was downright short of decent. His midsection tightened in an unconscious response to the invitation he saw in her eyes. As flattered as he was to have such a beauty take notice of him, he forced himself to glance away. There was something decidedly unsettling about the woman and her brother.

Adam met Amanda's hopeful look and hesitated. Why was she so determined to do this? Amanda had done some pretty crazy things in her time, but she had always listened to reason, especially when it came from him. Now he had a feeling if he didn't let her do this, she would find a way to get around him on her own, she was that stubborn. It was better if he could be there to keep an eye on her.

"There are the other drivers to consider," he told them.

"They would still receive their pay, don't worry about that," Mr. Dailey interrupted. "What if you went along as second conductor after you reach the Pike Rail Road? At each station, the relief driver who knows the route would take over, but you and Miss Ross would replace the regular conductor for the full journey. Do you think that would work?"

The Butterfield Overland Mail must really be running in the red if Mr. Dailey was that desperate. He looked at Adam with the same kind of hopeful expression as Amanda. Adam knew this wasn't going to work, but her violet eyes were working their old-time charm. He sighed heavily, irritated by his inability to reason rationally when it was obvious this was so important to Amanda.

There was a reason he had left home at seventeen, and he was looking at it. He had been unable to deny Amanda anything, and he knew the potential for some kind of disaster only grew with the passage of years. It was only a matter of time before her childish pranks would become more serious. It had never occurred to him she would someday follow *him* and prove that supposition.

"All right," he capitulated reluctantly, hoping he could still talk some sense into her.

Four pairs of eyes fixed on him in differing degrees of relief.

"But only if I am certain no harm will come to Amanda," he qualified.

"Excuse me, please."

Surprised at the quiet interruption, everyone turned to the man who had been silently studying the stage schedule. He was rather nondescript, someone who would easily be overlooked in a crowd. His plain black suit and round wire-rimmed glasses gave one the impression he was a businessman, but something about the man didn't quite fit the picture. Adam couldn't explain it; it was just something that set his instincts roiling.

"I couldn't help overhearing your conversation. Will

other passengers be allowed to ride this stagecoach that Mr. Nightington has commandeered? I have a ticket for Thursday, as well, and I really must get to California."

Mr. Dailey glanced at Evan Nightington. "That's true. Mr. Bass here and two other passengers have already booked passage for Thursday. You'll have to wait until Monday since no one has booked that stage."

Evan and Rose exchanged lightning glances. Rose gave an imperceptible nod of the head that Adam would have missed if he hadn't been looking at her instead of her brother. There was no doubt in his mind who was in charge in that family.

"We have no problem with that," Evan told them. "At least with only the five of us inside the coach, we will have a little leg room."

"Then it's settled," Mr. Dailey said, his smile reaching from ear to ear.

Adam caught the look the other passenger was giving the Nightingtons and was startled at the intensity of his stare. There was something almost sinister in his eyes. The man quickly glanced away when Evan turned to him, making Adam wonder about the man's connection to the Nightingtons—and just what exactly Adam had gotten himself and Amanda into.

Chapter 2

Amanda hurried from the Butterfield office, assuring Mr. Dailey—after he gave her written instructions on a conductor's duty—that she would be ready to leave on Thursday. Walking as quickly as she could, the paper clutched tightly in her fist, she tried to put as much distance between herself and Adam before he could escape from the agent, who was giving him an earful, as she had scuttled out of the office.

She should have known better. The sound of stomping boots behind her informed her Adam's long stride was eating up the distance between them. Sighing, she stopped and turned to face him.

He drew up in front of her, his eyes darkened almost to ebony by boiling rage. She swallowed hard, knowing the fury was directed at her. Although she had made him angry enough at times while growing up, having done something he thought was foolish, he had never looked at her like this.

"What?" It took a bit of doing to make the one-word question sound defiant.

Pedestrians hurrying along the board walkway that ran the length of the busy street bumped into them as they stood unmoving, glaring at each other. Gritting his teeth, Adam snatched her by the arm and marched her away.

Amanda tried to tug her arm from his grip, but he was unyielding. She took three steps to his one and, as it was, he was almost carrying her.

"Where are we going?" she demanded in irritation, trying desperately to keep the unease out of her voice. If Adam thought for one minute he could browbeat her, he had another think coming.

"We're going somewhere we can talk before I contact your father."

The defiance drained out of her. She meekly allowed him to drag her along, hoping that when they got where they were going, some of his ire would have abated and she could reason with him. In his present frame of mind, she hadn't a hope of doing so.

He finally stopped at a nearby restaurant. The area was fairly empty, since breakfast was long past and lunch had yet to begin. The muted sound of clinking silverware penetrating the closed doors separating the kitchen from the dining area was the only noise that would interrupt their discussion.

Despite his obvious irritation, Adam held a chair for her to take her seat, and she had to admire his manners. He might look like a character from the wild backwoods but, like her, he had been brought up by affluent parents who expected him to eventually take his rightful place in society. His etiquette was as ingrained in him as his love for the wild, open spaces that her uncle had imbued them both with. Two opposite ends of the social strata rolled into one impressive man. Civilized and uncivilized. She could only hope the civilized one would win out when it came to controlling his anger.

Amanda sniffed appreciatively at the odors wafting out when the waitress emerged from the kitchen to take their orders; a loud growl from her stomach was audible in the almost oppressive silence. Adam's mouth twitched slightly.

"When was the last time you ate?" he asked.

She knew better than to dissimulate. Adam had always been able to read her like a book.

"Yesterday at breakfast," she said grudgingly.

His lips pressed together in a tight line, his nostrils flaring. Giving a heavy exhale, he shook his head slowly from side to side, his searching look leaving her feeling suddenly defenseless.

He waited impatiently while the waitress listed off the available specials, and then placed his order, ignoring the menu placed before him.

Amanda hid a grin. Adam was totally unaware of the young waitress's efforts to engage his attention. She straightened her apron, patting her dark hair into place while trying to catch his eye.

It had always been thus, even during their school years. Something about Adam inspired confidence in a woman, and that kind of charisma was an attractive trait for a man to have. And from her experience, it was very rare. Yes, when the Good Lord created Adam, he definitely threw away the mold.

She returned Adam's study, noting he was handsomer than ever. She had seen him only a handful of times since he'd left home almost nine years ago. But they had kept in contact, though her letters outweighed his by ten to one. Except in the past two years when his letters had ceased altogether.

"And for you, sir?" The waitress interrupted Amanda's thoughts without taking her gleaming brown eyes off Adam's imposing figure.

Hot color flooded Amanda's cheeks. She looked up at

the waitress to correct her, but decided not to bother. Her whole purpose in dressing this way had been to be mistaken for a man. That she was obviously effective should make her feel proud of herself; instead it made her feel suddenly embarrassed and ashamed. It was dishonest, and she had been brought up to believe that subterfuge was a sin.

Instead, she quietly removed her hat, allowing her hair to tumble down her back in a mass of brown curls. The waitress's eyes widened, and she stared hard at Amanda. Even with her luxurious crown of hair, Amanda's plain features could easily be mistaken for those of someone less feminine.

The waitress coughed slightly, her face flushed with embarrassment. "I apologize...ma'am."

Amanda quietly nodded, accepting the apology, and then placed her order, certain the food would now choke her. She sipped a drink of water in the hopes it would dislodge the tight knot in her throat. She caught Adam's look and he lifted a dark brow, amusement lurking behind the anger in the depths of his shimmering eyes.

After the waitress left, Adam demanded, "Let's have it. Do your parents even know where you are?"

Amanda fidgeted with the silverware. She peeped at him from under lowered eyes, trying to gauge whether some of his anger had lessened and whether he was as yet in a malleable mood. The coldness had returned to his eyes, assuring her he was not.

"They know I'm in Memphis," she told him.

He leaned back in his chair, arms folded across his chest. He continued to stare at her without speaking, and she swallowed hard, recognizing the look for what it was. Only Adam could put so much into a look.

"All right, they think I'm staying with Aunt Lucinda."

He blinked, momentarily caught off guard. "Where *are* you staying?"

She hesitated. "At the Gayoso," she said reluctantly.

His eyes went wide. "You chose the most exclusive hotel in Memphis?"

She fiddled with her napkin, looking no higher than the leather ties of his buckskin shirt. "I thought it might be my only chance to experience such luxury and, besides, I figured Father would never think to look for me there if he checks with Aunt Lucinda and finds me missing."

There was that look again. She rolled her eyes, sighing. "All right. I told my parents I wanted to stay with Aunt Lucinda and go to the new dance studio that will be teaching all the newest dances from Europe."

He unfolded his arms, leaning them on the table to bring his face closer to hers. His eyes were almost black again. "You lied."

The disappointment in his voice made her feel lower than a worm.

"Not exactly," she hedged, taking another drink to keep from looking him in the eye. "There really is a dance studio opening that will be doing just that."

He sat back, folding his arms again in that nerve-racking manner of his. "Will be?"

"It opens in October."

The scriptures were clear on lying; she knew that, yet she had still perpetrated this whole scheme without giving much thought to the consequences. Adam had every right to be disappointed in her; she was disappointed in herself.

She heard his soft snort but, before he could say anything, she took the bull by the horns. "I had to, Adam. I had to try. I'm tired of being treated like a child, or worse, a little doll that will break if it's taken out of its package. I'm nineteen years old, and what have I done with my life?" She looked down to avoid his censure, fiddling with the silver fork. "Besides, if the Good Lord wanted to stop me, He could have."

* * *

Adam thought if he heard the term *Good Lord* one more time, he would possibly do Amanda an injury, but his anger was quickly replaced by understanding coupled with irritation. "Manny," he said gruffly, using the nickname he had branded her with years ago, "it's only because we care about you."

"I know that, Adam." She sighed. "But I'm not the sickly little child who almost died. I'm a grown woman. Haven't I proved myself capable time and time again?"

Adam remembered back to when he had first been introduced to Amanda. Her parents owned the plantation nearest his family, and their families had been friends for years.

He was seven years old when Amanda was born and, despite everyone else's excitement, he had found nothing to be excited about. Still, curiosity aroused, he had crept close to her cradle—and when no one was looking, he peeped inside to see what all the furor was about. Even then, her violet eyes had packed a punch. He had reluctantly stroked a finger gently across the downy softness of her cheek, marveling at its peach-fuzz smoothness. When her tiny little hand had clutched his finger so trustingly and she'd smiled up at him with those bright eyes, his heart had jumped into his throat. He had been her slave ever since.

Amanda had developed a fever when she was only three years old, which had affected her lungs and almost killed her. For years, she had to be treated with the utmost care. She had been horribly spoiled, but it was mainly because of her gentle personality that she was not so hard to live with—even if she did have a penchant for wanting her way. He had been as prone to give it to her as her parents.

It was inevitable their parents would try to force a match between Amanda and himself. The only problem was that he didn't see Amanda that way. She was like a little sister, and there wasn't anything in the world he wouldn't do for her. Except this scheme of wanting to be a Butterfield conductor. Regardless of what he had said earlier, he hoped to be able to talk her out of it without having to resort to physical means. He was not about to let her go trekking almost twenty-eight hundred miles across some of the roughest and most dangerous territory this country had to offer.

"Amanda," he remonstrated softly, "you might be able to shoot a gun better than most men, ride a horse like a circus performer and even crack a whip with expert ease, but that doesn't mean you are strong enough to face the rigors of the mail route."

"You, too, Adam?"

The way she said it, as though he was betraying her, was like a punch in the gut. He opened his mouth to protest, but she rushed on.

"I thought at least *you* would understand."

The waitress brought their food, leaning close when she set Adam's plate on the table. He hadn't paid much attention earlier, but now he saw the invitation in the young woman's eyes.

"Is there anything else I can do for you?" she asked, totally ignoring Amanda. He saw the amusement on Amanda's face and frowned.

"No, thank you."

She waited several seconds, but Adam refused to acknowledge her and she finally got the message and left.

"I think she likes you," Amanda teased, her violet eyes dancing with laughter. He was not amused.

"I prefer to do my own hunting, thank you. And stop trying to change the subject. What exactly do you mean you thought *I* would understand?"

She glared at him in obvious frustration. "You want

me to go back to being a dressed-up little doll, suffering through countless teas and parties until the right man comes along to increase my family's fortune, yet you have the freedom to ignore all the accoutrements of high society and be yourself. If you think it's so great, why don't you go home and take up your father's banking business like he wants you to?"

Thankfully, she ran out of breath. Her words had brought a bushel of guilt that he'd been trying hard to ignore for the past several years, and he didn't need her to remind him he was failing his family.

"I can do this, Adam," she whispered.

He didn't know what to say or what to do. Everything inside him told him this was foolishness. If anything were to happen to her...

After placing his napkin in his lap, he picked up his fork and knife and cut into the ham nestled in its bed of scrambled eggs. "Eat your food," he said roughly.

She hesitated but a second before following suit. They ate in silence for several minutes, Amanda appearing eager to fill an empty belly, and he lost in his own thoughts. Something she had said earlier came back to him now, and he laid his silverware on his plate with a decided clank.

"And for your information, you have never outshot me."

Amanda glanced up in surprise, the fork halfway to her mouth. Slowly, she returned the utensil to her plate. "Of course I have. Several times."

He continued to stare at her until his meaning finally registered. Her eyes went wide.

"You let me win?" she asked suspiciously.

Having gotten the message across, he picked up his fork and resumed eating. Out of the corner of his eye, he could see her sitting there staring at him, lips parted, chest heaving with ill-concealed irritation.

"You *let* me win!"

Her accusing voice made him flinch. He should have kept his mouth shut. Knowing Amanda, she would take it as some kind of challenge. His own irritation rose. He once again dropped the silverware to his plate. He pushed the dish aside, his hunger deserting him at the hurt look on her face.

He folded his arms on the table and leaned forward. "Why, Amanda? Why is this so important to you? Why do you always have to be proving yourself?"

She gave up her pretense of eating, as well. "You have to ask me that?"

Seeing a copy of *The Memphis Daily Appeal* lying on a deserted table nearby, she got up and retrieved it. Now what was she up to?

She flipped through the paper until she found the article she wanted. Folding the paper back, she slapped it on the table in front of him.

"There. Read that."

He glanced at her in surprise and then down at the paper. The title, "Fashionable Women," seemed innocuous enough. He picked up the paper and began reading.

Fashion kills more women than toil or sorrow. Uh-oh.

He glanced up and caught her smoldering look. Taking a breath, he resumed reading. Instead of supporting fashion in women, the article did just the opposite. It praised the longevity of life for slaves and working women, but then went on:

It is a sad truth that fashioned pampered women are almost worthless for all the great ends of human life. They have but little force of character; they have still less power of moral will, and quite as little physical energy. They live for no greater purpose in life; they accomplish no worthy ends. They are only doll forms in the hands of milliners and servants, to be dressed and fed to order.

The article continued, but he read no more. He threw the paper down on the table and glared at Amanda.

"Surely you don't believe that hogwash?"

"No, of course not," she denied, and then looked at her lap. "Well, maybe."

"Manny!"

She balled her fists, the frustration evident. "I don't know! Maybe it's true. Anyway, true or not, it's how I feel."

His frustration probably exceeded hers. "So you would risk your life, and the lives of six other people, to prove your point."

Her appalled look made him instantly regret that he had been so harsh. Before he could try to modify the statement, she fastened sorrowful violet eyes on him.

"You really don't think I can do it, do you? Despite what you said earlier. You lied, too."

He blew out a frustrated breath. "That's not true. I wouldn't have said it if I didn't believe it."

She continued to stare at him doubtfully. He leaned his elbows on the table, pushing his hands through his hair.

"All right," he conceded.

"All right, what?" she asked warily.

"All right, you can do it," he said sternly, "but you have to promise me one thing."

She leaned forward in her seat, her eyes now sparkling with excitement. "Anything."

"You have to promise that if it gets to be too much for you, you'll tell me."

"I promise," she told him readily.

He stared at her grimly, wondering if he had just lost his mind. He reached forward, extending a curled pinkie finger. She lifted surprised eyes to his, and then studied his finger as though it were a rattlesnake about to strike. It had always been their most solemn vow, and he knew that once given, she would never break it.

Her face was wreathed in indecision. Finally sighing in capitulation, she joined her curled pinkie with his.

"Pinkie promise," she agreed reluctantly.

Satisfied, he leaned back and studied her frowning face. "Now, what do we do about your folks?"

Chapter 3

They decided, for the time being, to allow things to stand as they were. Amanda knew her parents would eventually find out, but she hoped to be long gone when they did. Only when she and Adam were a safe distance away would she notify them. Ironically, by mail on the Butterfield stage since there was no telegraph service farther along the route.

She mostly regretted that her defiance and Adam's help in the matter would probably cause a rupture in the relationship between her family and Adam's. She was only now beginning to see the full import of what her impetuous actions might produce.

But it was Adam's few letters about life driving the Butterfield stage, and her uncle's stories of life on the frontier, that had inspired in her a longing to do something as dramatic with her own life.

Adam walked her to the door of her room at the Gayoso, waiting while she produced her key. Taking it from her, he opened the door and pushed it open.

He peered past her to the elegant interior of the room. "I hear they even have flush toilets."

Embarrassed, Amanda shook her head. "Adam! That's not an appropriate subject to be discussing with a lady."

She couldn't read the look that crossed his face. "Manny, if you're going to dress like a man and act like a man, then you need to be able to take it when you are treated as such."

Just one more thing she hadn't taken into consideration.

He gazed down at her, and she knew he was wrestling with his conscience.

Understanding his dilemma, she placed a hand on his arm and, lifting herself to her tiptoes, kissed him on the cheek.

"Thank you, Adam," she told him softly.

He inhaled sharply, closing his eyes and shaking his head. "I have to be out of my mind."

She met his wry smile with one of her own. "Not you. Me."

They stared into each other's eyes for several seconds, and Amanda felt an unfamiliar thrill course through her. Something in her look must have registered with Adam because his smile turned into a frown and he studied her curiously.

"Are you all right?" he asked.

She took a deep breath and shook off the odd feeling. "Fine." As she turned to go inside, something occurred to her. She turned back, cocking her head at him. "Where do you stay, Adam?"

It was so good to see his eyes their normally shifting hazel color and know that his anger had abated. At least for the time being.

"I rent a room from a very special lady who has fallen on hard times," he told her.

Could that little prism of feeling that sparked through her at the soft tone of his voice be jealousy? Surely not!

Adam was like her big brother. She certainly hoped she wasn't so selfish that she would deny Adam a female relationship.

"Here? In Memphis?" she asked.

He nodded, and she wondered how he could be so willing to live in a city when he loved the outdoors so much. As though she had asked the question, he said, "It's easier that way. Since I drive the first sixty miles of the mail route to Tipton, and then return on the stage coming from San Francisco, it made sense to have a place to keep my things for the days when I'm waiting for the next stage." He shrugged. "And it helps Maddie out."

She assumed Maddie was the woman who had fallen on hard times. It was just like Adam to help someone who needed it. She wondered just exactly how old this Maddie was.

The sound of someone thundering up the stairs caught their attention. A young boy slid to a halt in front of them. "Are you Adam?"

Adam's eyebrows winged upward. "I am."

"Mr. Dailey wants you and the…." He stopped, wrinkling his forehead in confusion. "The *lady*?"

Openmouthed, he gawked at Amanda's hair, which cascaded in luxurious brown curls down the back of her buckskin jacket. The jacket was a smaller replica of Adam's that he had purchased for her on one of his many travels. The boy blinked his eyes rapidly, and Amanda hid a grin at his obvious discomfort.

"You were saying?" Adam asked wryly.

The boy blinked again, squinting at Adam in confusion. "Huh?"

"You were saying?" This time the intonation of Adam's voice let the boy know he was fast losing patience.

The messenger glanced back at Amanda. "Oh, yeah." He smiled at her, and Adam's face darkened. He stepped between them, blocking the boy's view. Amanda stared at his rigid back in wonder. As she had reacted earlier, Adam seemed almost jealous, as well. As quickly as the thought occurred, she shook her head. No, that couldn't be; he was just being his normal, overprotective self.

She heard the boy say, "Mr. Dailey wants to see you both at his office as soon as possible."

When the messenger was finally out of view, Adam turned back to her.

"Shall we go and see what he wants?"

On the way to Dailey's office, Amanda felt little butterflies cavorting in her stomach. If Dailey had changed his mind, she didn't know what she would do. In all honesty, she was amazed at her own determination to see this through. Adam didn't have to ask her why; she was busy asking herself that question.

They found Dailey studying the route map on the wall of his office. As usual, the door was open, probably to allow more of the weak sunlight into the rather dark interior.

He turned to them as they entered. His craggy eyebrows wrinkled above light, indiscernible-colored eyes. His mustache moved up and down as he pressed his lips together.

He looked at Adam. "Not that I doubt your word, but I decided I needed a little more proof of Miss Ross's abilities."

Adam's eyes narrowed. "What kind of proof?"

Dailey snatched his hat and coat from the peg on the wall by the door. He twirled the hat in his hands, motioning with his head for them to precede him out the door.

For the first time, Amanda noticed the wagon parked on the street outside. She glanced at Dailey when he motioned to the driver's seat.

"You can drive," he told her.

Adam's hands curled into fists at his side, but he said nothing.

Amanda scrambled into the driver's seat, and Dailey climbed up beside her. Grabbing the sides of the wagon, Adam nimbly vaulted into the back.

The butterflies in Amanda's stomach had turned into a churning storm. She glanced hesitantly at Adam and gained confidence from his look of approbation. He nodded, and she took a deep breath, reaching for the reins at the same time. It wasn't the first time she had driven a wagon, so she didn't doubt her ability to do so now. But it was a little different driving on the busy streets of Memphis compared with the wide-open plantation fields back home.

The seat creaked when she turned to her new boss. "Where to?" she asked, trying to instill a confidence in her voice that she was far from feeling at this moment.

He nodded forward. "Just head on down Main Street. I'll tell you when to turn."

Adam leaned close, and Amanda could sense his tension. "Where are we going?"

"You'll see."

Mr. Dailey said no more except to give directions. After what seemed like hours, Amanda noticed they were nearing the outskirts of the teeming city, houses and businesses becoming more sporadic the closer they got to the country beyond.

They were well beyond the city limits when Dailey asked her to pull the wagon off the road. They bumped along the grass-covered area until Dailey ordered her to stop.

The faint sound of a far-off steamboat whistle broke the ensuing silence. Birds chattered in the nearby woods.

Dailey climbed down from the wagon and moved to stand beside the team of horses. He glanced back at them with a cocked eyebrow. Adam exchanged a look with Amanda before, shrugging his shoulders, he followed suit.

Before she could climb down on her own, Adam reached up and wrapped his hands around her waist to help her from the wagon. Her questioning look reminded him of their earlier conversation, and color stole up his neck and across his face.

"No matter how you dress or how you act," he snapped, "you will always be a lady to me."

The feeling that had surged through her earlier shivered through her again, only now increased tenfold. She settled her hands on his shoulders, feeling his muscles bunch as he lifted her down.

Adam set her on her feet and frowned into her eyes. He slowly removed his hands from her waist, and even though he didn't move away, the distance between them seemed to increase.

Dailey stepped to the back of the wagon and, reaching inside, pulled out a Sharps rifle. He threw it to Amanda, who barely had time to react before she instinctively caught it.

"Let's see what you've got," he told her and, coming to stand beside her, handed her a small bag containing several paper shot shells.

She set the bag on the wagon seat and lifted the gun, the familiar feel of the rifle in her hands giving her confidence, as well as bringing back happy memories.

Her uncle had visited their home often when she was growing up. His tales of the mountains and frontier life had whetted her appetite for adventure, and had set Adam on the path that he was treading now.

Her mother hadn't really approved of Father's brother, but Uncle Taylor and Father had always been close. Uncle Taylor was actually the oldest son, but had forsaken his inheritance to test his freedom on the frontier. He had never regretted it. Because Amanda trailed her uncle about like a shadow when he visited, he had secretly taught her to do things that would have appalled her parents.

Her hero worship of Uncle Taylor had been one of the biggest factors contributing to her refusal to accept the role that had been dictated to her. Especially since *he* was free of so many of the restrictions and conventions that fenced her in. She often slipped away from the house and into the woods to practice throwing her Bowie knife and cracking her whip until she was almost as good as Uncle Taylor.

When Adam had caught her with a gun, he had taken it upon himself to show her how to load it and shoot properly. She had suffered through many bruised shoulders until she had learned to toughen up and hold the gun correctly.

Every day she had snuck away to the woods close to their plantation near Nashville. Adam would meet her there and together they both practiced, often setting up contests between them.

She looked at him now, remembering that he had said she had never outshot him. The amusement in his eyes, coupled with the confidence she saw in his face, had a settling effect on her dancing nerves.

She quickly took the powder cartridge, loading it into the breech. When she had finished, she glanced at Mr. Dailey. "Do you have a target in mind?"

His look of admiration lifted her spirits considerably. Coming close, he pointed to a small sapling about four hundred yards in the distance at the very edge of the forest. Dropping his arm, he glanced at her doubtfully.

"Do you think you can hit that?"

She looked at Adam, and he nodded his head reassuringly.

Tucking the butt of the gun into the cusp of her shoulder, and using the bed of the wagon to steady the heavy barrel, she carefully sighted in on the spindly tree Mr. Dailey had indicated. Taking a deep breath, she held it while she made sure of her sight. She slowly squeezed the trigger, and the rifle fired, the shot flying unerringly to its target, splitting the thin trunk of the tree and snapping it in half.

Amanda pressed her lips together to keep from grinning at Mr. Dailey's look of shocked amazement, and to hide the grimace of pain—her shoulder hurt from the kick of the rifle.

She glanced at Adam and saw the twinkle mixed with pride in his eyes.

"Satisfied?" he asked the other man.

"Impressed," Mr. Dailey replied, "but not yet satisfied." He nodded his head at the Remington double-action revolver peeking from its holster beneath the edge of her buckskin coat. "How good are you with that?"

He pulled an empty whiskey bottle from the back of the wagon and pitched it several yards away, where it rolled onto the ground. The whole world seemed to hold its breath as Amanda focused on the brown glass. Inhaling deeply, she tucked her coat behind her holster, unlatching the leather safety strap.

After years of practicing, instinct took over and with one quick movement, she drew the gun from its holster, firing off five shots in quick succession, shattering the bottle into small shards.

Mr. Dailey stared in disbelief at the broken bottle. Brushing away the smoking sulfur floating in the air, he cleared his throat.

"Are you satisfied now?" Adam asked, his smug look of pride in her ability making Amanda feel as if she were twenty feet tall.

Mr. Dailey shook his head, rubbing his temple. "I've never seen anything like it." He addressed her with new respect. "You must have been practicing for years!"

That was putting it mildly. "You have no idea, but as

the Good Lord says, if you're going to do something, do it right and with all your might."

She heard Adam's snort, but ignored him, concentrating on Mr. Dailey instead.

He grinned at her comment, his eyes glued to the gun. "May I see that weapon?"

Amanda handed him the revolver, reminding herself she would need to clean it and reload the cylinder. He carefully inspected the gun. "I've never seen a weapon like this. Where did you get it?"

Amanda felt a rush of remorse. In fact, she had absconded with it from her father's collection. The revolver was a new prototype that had been patented only a little over a year ago. It had rapidly become a favorite of hers because of its size and lightness. Goodness knew what her father was going to say when he found it missing.

"It's my father's," she finally answered, catching Adam's look of disapproval. He rolled his eyes and shook his head, making her guilt intensify.

"And where did your father get it?"

Amanda took back the pistol from him, twirling it and flipping it back into its holster with expert ease. "My father is a gun connoisseur. Since he sits on the legislature, he has an inside source when new weapons become available."

"I'd sure like to get my hands on one of those," Mr. Dailey said, moving to the wagon and pulling himself up to the front seat.

Amanda followed him, smiling when Adam held out his hand to help her up. Despite his pride in her ability, he didn't return her smile. Something was bothering him.

When everyone was situated, Amanda picked up the reins and turned the horses, about to retrace their steps.

No one spoke as they made their way back to the city, all of them busy with their own thoughts. Amanda stopped the wagon in front of the Butterfield office, and they quickly climbed down.

Mr. Dailey removed his hat from his head. "I'll see you Thursday, then, Miss Ross."

She let out the breath she didn't even know she had been holding. "Thank you, sir."

He entered his office, leaving Amanda and Adam on the boardwalk outside. Adam lifted an eyebrow at her.

"I may have let you win before, but I'll know better next time."

Amanda grinned at him, warmed by his sincere praise. "I had the best teacher."

Adam threw an arm around her shoulder. "Come on. I'll buy you lunch. I don't know about you, but I'm starving."

Since they had both been too upset to finish their earlier breakfast, so was she.

He took her back to the restaurant where they had breakfasted earlier. Since it was lunchtime, the place was crowded. Amanda accidentally bumped into a man and he turned to her with a glare.

"Watch where you're going, bud," he snarled, shoving her to the side.

Adam stepped forward, his eyes glittering dangerously. Amanda pushed in front of him, taking his attention from the other man.

"Leave it, Adam."

He glared at her, then back at the other man, who had already turned away. His nostrils flared as he sucked in a breath to curb his quickly fired temper. He gave her a brief nod to let her know he understood and they moved on to an empty table in the corner.

A different waitress attended them this time, and she was much too busy to take note of the customers, although she did do a double take when she took Adam's order.

After she left, Adam leaned back in his chair. "Your father is going to kill you."

He didn't mean literally, but she got the gist of his thoughts. "Disown me, maybe," she agreed.

He leaned forward, placing his arms on the table, and she could see her reflection in his darkened pupils. "Give this up, Amanda, and go home where you belong."

Adam wanted to reach across the table and shake Amanda until her common sense returned. His hands curled into fists at the thought. He was so frustrated he didn't know what to do.

Yes, she could shoot a small sapling at four hundred paces and split it in two. Yes, she could shatter a bottle with five perfect shots. Yes, he had no doubts she could handle a stagecoach if needed, but this was not the safe haven of her father's plantation or the thriving city of Memphis. This was going to be some of the roughest territory this country had to offer, with renegade Apaches and thieving bandoleros. This was serious business.

When her face filled with distress at his seeming rejection, he gritted his teeth and studied the ceiling, where he at least had a respite from her luminous wounded eyes. He sighed heavily.

"Manny, I'm not saying you couldn't handle the job. I just don't want anything to happen to you."

Her eyes glittered with emotion. When they turned that specific shade of plum, he knew she was on the boil.

"What about you, Adam? If it's so dangerous, what about you? Do you think I don't worry about you? Do you think I don't care?"

"In the first place," he said, stopping when the waitress interrupted with their food. She placed a plate of fried chicken, fried potatoes and glazed carrots in front of him and then one in front of Amanda. She then poured them each a cup of coffee.

"Can I get you anything else?"

She barely waited for his negative shake of the head before she hurried to the next table.

Adam turned back to Amanda.

"As I was saying. In the first place, I only drive the route from here to Tipton, and that is safe, clear roads." He picked up his fork, leveling it in her direction. "Hardly dangerous."

He scooped up a forkful of potatoes, stopping halfway to his mouth when he saw the look on her face. He set the fork down and frowned.

"What's the matter?"

She blinked rapidly to stem the moisture forming in her eyes. Heavens above, if she started crying, he would be lost for sure.

"Play fair, Amanda!" he practically growled.

"Oh, Adam. I wasn't thinking." She pushed her plate away, her face so doleful he had to bite his tongue to keep from rescinding his earlier objection.

"No, Manny. You never do," he agreed softly.

She placed her small hand over his larger one, and he felt a jolt that nearly took his arm off. She must have felt it, too, because her eyes widened in surprise, the confusion in them mirroring the emotions stampeding through him, as well.

She quickly removed her hand, curling it into a fist against her chest.

"Do you think it's too late to back out?" she asked. "I never meant to get you involved in something that could get you killed."

He wanted to whoop with joy. Instead, he attempted a sorrowful look with just the right amount of forgiveness.

"I'm sure Mr. Dailey would be willing to let you out of this deal. After all, you didn't sign any contract."

She straightened in her seat, giving him the impression of a rattlesnake about to strike.

"I meant *you*," she informed him, a defiant gleam in her eyes. "I have every intention of going through with this *deal*, as you call it."

His own defiance rose to meet hers. "If I quit, Mr. Dailey will have to call it off."

"Wanna bet?" she asked. "With ten thousand dollars on the line, would you? The Good Lord says whoever loves money never has enough. It would take something more serious than your defection to make Mr. Dailey give up ten thousand dollars."

His hands curled into fists again, and Amanda hurriedly moved his plate out of his reach. "Now, now," she cajoled, her eyes filling with suppressed amusement. "Mind your manners."

"Manners be hanged!" he ground out, but the reminder had the desired effect, and he swallowed the fury practically choking him.

Amanda played with her fork, peeking at him from under lowered lashes. "We can do this, Adam. You and me together. Just like always."

The fury ebbed away to be replaced by something he would rather not try to discern at the moment.

"I gave you my word," she reminded him. "Pinkie promise. Besides, God will be watching over us. He's never failed me yet."

Did she even consider that her actions were contrary to her professed beliefs? But who was he to judge? He would need to trust her, and that belief that was such a part of her, because he had lost his own faith some time ago.

He stared at her for several seconds before he once again reached for his fork. Shaking his head, he told her,

"Eat your food. It might be the last good meal you get for some time."

The tense atmosphere between them eased as it always did whenever she managed to sway him to her way of thinking.

Picking up her fork, she flashed him a brilliant smile.

Her dad was going to kill him, and this time he meant it literally.

Chapter 4

Amanda was awakened by a loud pounding on her door. Gray light filtered through the window's drawn shades, and she squinted, trying to make out the time on the clock, which hung on the wall.

She tumbled out of bed to stand, disoriented, in the middle of the floor in her chemise and drawers, her hair hanging in wild abandon around her shoulders. Her toes curled against the chilly temperatures of the wood floor. Trying to bring her thoughts into focus, she almost growled when the pounding resumed.

"Who is it?"

"Adam."

She gasped quietly and crossed her arms over her chest as though he could see through the wooden portal.

"Just…just a minute!"

Quickly surveying the room, she grabbed a quilt from the bed, hastily wrapping it around herself. Padding to the door in her bare feet, she warily opened it only as far as the chain would allow.

She glared at him through the small space.

"Are you out of your mind? Do you know what time it is?" she hissed, trying not to awaken the occupants of the nearby rooms, although if they could sleep through Adam's drubbing on her door, they could sleep through anything.

"I do. Do you?" he greeted cheerfully. His look slid over her tousled appearance and she saw his lips twitch. "Why are you wearing a quilt?"

Ignoring the question, she asked one of her own. "Why are you here, Adam? It's barely daylight."

He grinned at her surly tone. "Ah. I remember now. You're not a morning person."

She fixed him with an eloquent eye. "I repeat. Why are you here?"

He folded his arms across his chest in that stoical way of his, one dark eyebrow lifting at her rudeness. "I thought, if you would like, we might have breakfast together at Maddie's, and then I'll show you around Memphis. Maddie would like to meet you."

Maddie. The widow who had fallen on hard times yet managed to support herself by running a boardinghouse. Yes, come to think of it, Amanda *would* like to meet her, as well. And frankly, she could think of nothing she would like better than spending the day with Adam and finding out where he had been for the past two years.

"Let me get dressed and I'll be right with you," she said.

She wondered just exactly what he was thinking when he looked at her in that odd way, his hazel eyes gleaming with amusement. "I'll wait for you downstairs."

Amanda didn't close the door until she saw him turn and walk away, wondering at the feeling of happiness that surged through her, making her want to dance across the room. For a moment, she stood motionless, grinning from ear to ear.

Throwing the quilt back onto the bed, she hurriedly pulled a clean shirt from her valise and slipped it on. She donned her buckskin outfit after removing it from the hook on the back of the door. Although the room boasted an armoire, she preferred to allow the leather to air overnight. It had a tendency to absorb body odors when not given a proper airing.

She picked up her brush to give her hair a quick once-over, but hesitated at the reflection staring back at her. Something was different. The same violet eyes, freckled nose and oversize mouth that she saw every day stared back at her, yet something had decidedly altered, something she couldn't put a name to.

Frowning at her fanciful thoughts, she grabbed the key from the dresser and, shoving it into the inside pocket of her jacket, pushed her hair once again under the confines of her hat and hurried to join Adam.

He stood next to the fountain that bubbled in the center of the main lobby, lost in thought. She paused, the jump to her heart bringing a quick frown to her face. What was the matter with her, anyway? She had always been happy to see Adam, yes, but this thrumming of her pulse each time they were together was a new addition.

He looked up and caught her gaze, and the thrumming intensified until Amanda thought her heart was about to fly out of her chest. Seeing her hesitation, a frown formed on Adam's face, which she thought matched the one she hurriedly smoothed from her own face.

She crossed the elegant foyer to join him at the fountain and smiled up at him. "I'm ready."

He didn't immediately respond. The furrow between his brows failed to retreat until, after several seconds, she cocked her head in question. Whatever thoughts were bothering him, he shook them off, giving her the grin she remembered so well.

"Let's go, then." Taking her by the arm, he guided her out of the hotel and into the early-morning mist that floated up from the warm water of the Mississippi River.

"Is that all you have to wear?" he asked.

Her eyes scanned his similarly buckskin-clad form. "Is there a problem?" she asked coolly. If this was about impressing his friend Maddie, and Maddie couldn't accept her as she was, then Amanda really wasn't interested in meeting her after all.

"Well...I thought we might spend the day together seeing the sights and, then, possibly attend the theater tonight."

She stared at him, nonplussed. She had been so focused on escaping the plantation without notice, and playing the part she had set for herself, she hadn't considered it a necessity to bring any clothes other than those she had with her now.

"It's not exactly feasible to carry a crinoline petticoat in a small valise," she retorted wryly. The hoops and stays of the bell-shaped undergarment practically needed a trunk of their own.

Adam stopped short and gaped at her in surprise. "Since when did you start wearing hoops and stays?"

Amanda's face colored hotly as his raised voice brought several stares their way. The middle of a busy city street was nowhere to be having such a personal discussion. Those who had heard his question glared at them balefully as they passed. Adam was ignoring just about all of the rules of street etiquette.

Amanda smiled lamely at the passing people while muttering under her breath, "Not here, Adam."

Realizing they had an audience, he looked around and

gave back glare for glare until the people hurried away shaking their heads.

"You know, they probably consider you a heathen, if not a downright savage," she told him, lips twitching.

He took her by the arm and began walking again. "Let them think what they like."

It was hard to believe this was the same Adam who had frequently instructed her on street etiquette. She had never seen him like this. It was unlike him to be so neglectful of proper decorum, and especially with a woman. Was he, because of her dress and actions, starting to see her as something less than the proper and genteel lady she had been brought up to be? The thought concerned her, making her once again question the wisdom of her actions.

A shiver that had nothing to do with the chilly morning air made goose bumps skip along her skin despite the warmth of her hide clothing.

After walking several blocks in silence, Adam stopped in front of a large house that in earlier times had probably been one of Memphis's finest. It still gave an imposing impression of wealth, with its high porch columns extending two stories high, despite the sign over the door that read Maddie's Boardinghouse, and the obvious neglect of the front yard.

Adam knocked on the front door and opened it, calling, "Maddie, we're here." He placed a hand on Amanda's back, ushering her inside.

She sniffed appreciatively at the smells wafting down the long hallway that extended to the back of the house. Her mouth watered at the scent of cinnamon intermingled with cooking ham. She glanced about her as Adam led her toward what she assumed was the kitchen.

Although the outside of the house was somewhat shabby, the inside was understated elegance. Amanda recognized the porcelain vases holding bouquets of mums as some of the finest Italian import. The paradox left her curious about this woman who, when Adam spoke of her, infused a warmth to his voice that she had rarely heard him use.

A little elderly woman appeared from the back of the house, wiping her hands on a small linen towel. Amanda was surprised at the overwhelming sense of relief she felt.

The woman's black hooped skirt swayed as she walked toward them, her bright blue eyes twinkling merrily as she studied Amanda with apparent curiosity. She patted the gray curls on the side of her face into already perfect order. Holding out a hand, she smiled at Amanda.

"How do you do? It's so nice to meet a friend of Adam's."

"Likewise," Amanda agreed, taking the proffered hand and dropping into a curtsy. Though thin and blue-veined, Maddie's hand held a strength that surprised Amanda. She and Maddie studied each other, both seeming to like what they saw.

Adam's lips twisted, and it occurred to Amanda that it was a little ludicrous to be practicing the manners of a well-brought-up lady when dressed like a man. Her cheeks blossomed with color, causing the grin on Adam's face to widen.

Adam placed an arm around the old woman's shoulder and drew her closer. "Maddie, this is Amanda. Amanda, Maddie is the best cook this side of the Mississippi."

Maddie's wrinkled cheeks pinkened with embarrassed pleasure, adding a youthful look to her aging face. She swatted Adam playfully on the arm.

"Oh, go on with you." Her vivid blue eyes twinkled at Amanda, their lovely color a reminder of a once-beautiful woman. It wasn't hard to imagine her in the role of gracious debutante. "Adam has told me a lot about you," she said, smiling.

"Has he?" Amanda eyed Adam doubtfully, but he simply chuckled, refusing to enlighten her.

"Oh, yes," Maddie replied, tucking her arm into Amanda's and guiding her back in the direction she had just come from. "I always hoped to one day meet you. Adam speaks very highly of you."

Amanda threw Adam a curious look over her shoulder, and he shrugged, following along behind.

Instead of the kitchen, Maddie led them to the dining room, which contained an already-set table. A blazing fire in the fireplace gave not only warmth to the room, but ambiance, as well. Crystal goblets and Wedgwood china added to the house's overall atmosphere of elegance.

"Have a seat," Maddie said, and Adam held Amanda's chair for her. She slid into the Queen Anne chair, staring about her in wonder. No one would expect such elegance from the outside of the house, and she had never seen a boardinghouse that boasted this kind of sophistication.

Adam seated himself, and Maddie disappeared through a door that Amanda assumed led to the kitchen.

She returned a moment later bearing a platter of cooked ham and scrambled eggs. After setting them on the table, she disappeared again only to return with a pan of warm cinnamon rolls.

"Help yourself," she told them, "while I get the coffee." She looked inquiringly at Amanda. "Or would you rather have tea?"

"Actually, I'd rather have milk if you have any."

"Plain, or butter?"

"Plain, please."

Nodding, Maddie left and came back with the milk. She set it in front of Amanda and poured a cup of coffee for Adam and herself. He jumped up to hold out her chair for her, and she took her place at the head of the table,

Amanda on her right and Adam on her left. She thanked Adam with a smile.

"Would you care to ask God's blessing?" she asked Amanda. When Amanda glanced uncomfortably at Adam, Maddie waved a hand. "I've never been able to get Adam to do so."

Amanda's lips parted in surprise, and color rushed into Adam's face. He had always been a godly young man; what had happened to him that he was unwilling to ask a simple grace? His look warned her not to ask.

She willingly bowed her head and asked the blessing on the fragrant food, adding a second, silent request that she would be able to find out what had happened to change Adam so much.

"So tell me," Maddie began when Amanda finished, taking a biscuit and adding it to her plate, "why are you running away from home and in such an unconventional way?"

Amanda almost choked on her mouthful of eggs. She frowned at the other woman and thought about telling her it was none of her business, but something about Maddie's face showed her honest concern, and Amanda's ire fled as swiftly as it had surfaced.

Adam watched her carefully. "I'd be interested to know that myself."

Amanda glanced from one to the other, reluctant to confide in a total stranger. Her gaze finally rested on Adam when she said, "My father has arranged a marriage for me that I don't wish to enter into."

Adam's mouth dropped, his fork clanging against the plate and making Amanda wince. She hoped he hadn't chipped the beautiful dinnerware.

"*What*? Who?" he demanded, the color in his face warning her that his explosive temper was on the rise.

She really hadn't planned to talk about this right now, but Adam's determined face demanded an answer. "Jedediah Stuart," she told him quietly, and his face darkened further.

He threw his napkin on the table and rose to his feet. His hazel eyes had once again turned black with emotion. "Over my dead body!"

Maddie glanced from one to the other, blinking in surprise. Apparently, she had never been privy to Adam's volatile temper.

"Now, Adam," she soothed, "let the girl have her say." She turned to Amanda. "I take it there's something objectionable about the young man?"

"Objectionable?" Adam snarled, his hands curling into fists at his side. The flickering candlelight coupled with the shifting patterns caused by the glow from the fire highlighted the strong angles of his face, giving him an ominous appearance. "He's rude, condescending, arrogant, brutish, selfish…" He stopped, apparently running out of appropriate adjectives. "How could your father even consider such a…a…?"

"You would have to ask my father," Amanda interjected, and she jutted her chin defiantly. "As you well know, we women have very little say-so in such matters."

"Bunkum!" he disagreed, his glittering eyes looking as though they were on fire with the reflected glow from the candle flames. "When have your parents ever made you do something against your wishes?"

When you disappeared from our lives, she wanted to shout. She glared at him helplessly, unable to put into words how much things had changed since he had left. Her whole world had turned upside down in the past few years.

"It's different now, Adam," she told him, frustrated. "I don't know why, but things have changed."

Adam edged himself back into his chair. The fear in Amanda's eyes was very real, and they contained not just dread, but downright panic. His whole thought process slowed, halted and did a 180-degree turn.

He would have to get to the bottom of this, but not until they were alone. No one objected when he changed the subject, keeping up a rambling discourse that lasted throughout the meal. Maddie wisely refrained from bringing up any more subjects that touched on Amanda's personal life.

When they finished their meal, Amanda offered to help with the dishes, but Maddie waved her away. "You and Adam go have some fun." She smiled at him. "I fixed the picnic basket you asked for. It's in the kitchen. I'll get it."

When the door closed behind her, Adam took a deep breath and blew it out slowly. "I'm sorry, Manny. I overreacted."

She sighed just as deeply. "Oh, Adam. I wished for you so many times. Father has changed and he won't tell me what's wrong." She brushed a hand through her hair in agitation. "After you left, everything seemed to go wrong."

He studied her seriously before getting up and crossing to her side. Squatting in front of her, he took both of her hands in his. Hers were like ice, and he knew it had nothing whatsoever to do with the weather. She looked so lost that his protective instincts swelled to alarming proportions.

Before he could say anything, Maddie returned, toting a small basket. Adam rose and took it from her.

"Thanks, Maddie."

She nodded, glancing at Amanda's white face and then back at Adam. "You take care of this little lady."

He knew she was referring to more than just today. Amanda was in trouble and, as usual, it was up to him to get her out of it.

"I will."

Amanda slowly got to her feet and smiled at Maddie, appearing reluctant to leave the woman's warm hospitality. "Thank you for breakfast, Maddie. I agree with Adam. You *are* the best cook this side of the Mississippi."

Maddie patted her cheek. "You come back anytime, hon. And if you need a place to stay next time, you just come on by. There's always room."

"I'll do that," Amanda agreed.

Adam motioned for her to precede him from the room and then from the house. As they walked down the crumbling stone porch steps, Adam took Amanda by the arm and squeezed reassuringly. She smiled up at him in appreciation, and he felt as though something jumped to life inside his chest. Whatever it was, he squelched it quite ruthlessly. Amanda was in trouble and it was no time to try to separate confusing feelings into neat little cubbyholes as he normally did when something troubled him.

"I've rented a buggy for the afternoon. I thought we would head out of town and find a spot near the Mississippi where we can have a nice little chat."

She didn't look exactly thrilled with the idea, but she allowed him to lead her to the livery stable at the end of town. The early-morning mist was already giving way under the rising sun.

The owner of the stable had the buggy ready, and Adam helped Amanda inside, irritated at the livery agent's curious stare. A man didn't need help into a buggy from another man. Adam took off Amanda's hat, allowing her hair to fall down her back in an abundant brown wave, and handed the head covering back to her.

She stared at him in surprise until she saw the stable owner's eyes widen in astonishment as he hastily removed his own hat, spitting a wad of tobacco juice on the ground. Adam watched her cheeks pinken in embarrassment when she realized the man hadn't seen through her disguise.

Adam picked up the reins, but hesitated. "You wanna drive?"

He couldn't begin to interpret the look she gave him, but it made him feel as though he had just crossed some kind of line he shouldn't have.

"No." She looked straight ahead. "You know the area better than I do."

Still, he hesitated. When she continued to avoid his eyes, he shrugged mentally and snapped the reins.

As they traveled, the cold February air warmed, dissipating the final fingers of fog. The sounds of the waking city faded as they put some distance between themselves and Memphis.

Amanda shivered.

"Are you cold?"

She shook her head, still refusing to look at him. "No. I'm fine."

She wasn't fine. Her whole attitude informed him he had done something seriously wrong, but he couldn't for the life of him figure out what. Before, she would have let him know in no uncertain terms what was bothering her, but now, something had imperceptibly changed between them and he didn't know how to get back to their earlier footing, or even if he wanted to. He frowned.

"Okay. What have I done?" he asked, slowing the team of horses until they were traveling along at a more sedate pace.

She glanced at him in sham surprise. "Nothing. Why do you ask?"

He wasn't fooled. He met her look squarely. "Manny, we've known each other all our lives. When I have done something wrong, you always have this particular…I don't know…air about you."

She looked as though she were about to deny it but then, cocking her head slightly, she asked him, "Adam, how do you see me?"

He jerked so hard on the reins, the horses shied before

stopping dead in the road. Exasperated, he snapped the straps to send them on their way again.

"What do you mean, how do I see you? What kind of question is that?"

"You said you will always see me as a lady." Her cheeks flushed. "Did you mean it?"

He watched her play with the fringe on her buckskin jacket. He didn't know why, but for some reason, she couldn't bring herself to look at him. It reminded him of when they were children and she would try to hide from him the fact she knew what he had gotten for Christmas.

Confused, he studied her face closely as he had in times past, trying to see behind the meaning of the words. "I meant it. Why do you ask?"

She shrugged, glancing everywhere but at him. "No reason."

And then it dawned on him. Is that what this was all about? He knew his opinion had always counted more to her than any other person, even her parents. Had he given the impression that he no longer thought of her as a lady because she wore buckskin and wanted to drive a stage? That was ridiculous. Despite her family's objections, she had been wearing buckskin clothing around the plantation ever since she was a child, thanks to her rather unusual uncle and parents who had never been able to say no to her.

Adam pulled off the road near the trees close by the river and stopped. Tying the reins to the buggy, he turned to her, placing an arm across the back of the seat.

"Manny," he tried, watching her face closely, "you will always be a lady. Don't you know that it's what's inside that matters the most?"

He watched her swallow hard and knew she was fighting back tears. "Oh, Adam! I don't know what I'm doing anymore!"

She buried her face in her hands, her shoulders shaking with quiet sobs.

Adam couldn't breathe. He hurt for her and didn't know what to say. He wrapped her in his arms and held her close, just as when they were younger and she ran to him whenever she was hurting. Only unlike those times, he was aware that she was no longer a child, but a young woman.

She clutched the front of his shirt, burying her head against his chest. He closed his eyes as he tried to take her pain upon himself.

"How about if we do this," he told her huskily. "We'll do as we planned and make this trip to San Francisco together and then, when we get back, I'll take you home and talk to your parents. How does that sound?"

She pulled back against his arm and smiled up into his face. Her tears had left her eyes blotchy, her nose red and weeping, but he still thought her as cute as the day she had stared up at him from her cradle.

Pulling his handkerchief from his pocket, he dried her face.

"Come on," he smiled. "Let's go watch the steamships."

That night, Amanda sat on the chair in front of the mirrored dresser in her chemise and pantalets and stared at her reflection without really seeing it.

It had been an unusual day. Originally, she'd had no intention of troubling Adam with her worries, but it had all come tumbling out as they watched the steamships and paddleboats trolling up and down the Mississippi.

Since her father was in the state legislature, talk of secession made him concerned there would soon be war. He had seemed to age overnight, and he had changed from the easygoing, loving man she had always known and loved to a tyrannical dictator. He had even gone so far as to threaten to destroy her beloved buckskins. That had been the last straw. It had felt like a betrayal.

She felt as if her life was a whirlpool and she was being sucked into an abyss. Truth to tell, she had felt that way ever since Adam had left years ago, as though he had taken the best part of her with him and her life had been spiraling out of control ever since.

Was she unjustly blaming him for her problems? Did she think that by bringing them back together everything would return to the way it was before?

She threw down her brush. Frankly, she wasn't certain she knew what she was doing anymore. All she knew was that she could not marry a man she didn't love just so she and her mother would have protection from the holocaust her father was expecting.

She couldn't fault her father for wanting to protect them, but she had to make him see that she could take care of herself if worse came to worst.

Shivering, she got up from her seat, crossed the room to the fireplace and stared into the flickering flames. The electric clock on the wall chimed nine times, and she knew she should get to bed. She had a long day ahead of her tomorrow. Her stomach clenched just thinking about it.

She watched the hands on the electromagnetic clock slowly ticking away the minutes, marveling at Alexander Bain's invention, which he had patented in 1840. Since the Gayoso Hotel was the most modern and up-to-date building of its time in Memphis, it boasted many amenities that even her father with all his wealth couldn't imagine.

The clock was run by a battery that made it unnecessary to wind it or pull the pendulum levers to keep it going. Amanda shook her head, amazed at all the newfangled items this hotel boasted. They surely lived in a marvelous time, but the threat that loomed over the whole country darkened her outlook considerably. Talk of secession and impending war had everyone on edge.

She finally retreated to bed, snuggling into the luxurious mattress and pulling the quilt over her. She picked up her Bible from the bedside table and, turning up the lamp, opened to Psalm 46, her very favorite Psalm.

God is our refuge and strength, a very present help in trouble. Therefore, will not we fear, though the earth be removed, and though the mountains be carried into the midst of the sea; though the waters thereof roar and be troubled, though the mountains shake with the swelling thereof.

The power of the words swept through her as they always did and brought her instant comfort.

It wasn't up to her to drive the stage, though she knew she could if she had to; it was up to her to see that the mail arrived in California on time.

Since Adam had only ever driven the first leg of the journey from Memphis to Fort Smith, he had to rely on the reports of the other drivers concerning the rest of the country. Rugged terrain, bandits, fierce Apache Indians, rattlesnakes, dust storms, raging rivers… She must be out of her mind!

Amanda reread Psalm 46 and allowed the words to soothe her once again. She could do this. With God to protect her, and Adam to guide her, she couldn't fail.

Placing the book back on the table, she turned down the lamp until the flame slowly disappeared, reducing the light to darkness. Her last thoughts were her prayers lifted upward from a grateful heart.

Chapter 5

Adam hitched the last horse to the stagecoach and patted its sable neck. Lifting the lantern, he walked around, checking once again the harnesses on all six horses, making certain they were tight.

His look traveled down the street as it had every few minutes for the past hour, watching for Amanda to appear, although it would be hard to see her in the early-morning darkness. In a way, he hoped she wouldn't show, but knowing Amanda as he did, he knew that was an impossibility. Once she set her mind on a course, she was as unstoppable as a herd of stampeding cattle.

When she finally appeared, it was under the streetlight on the corner down the block. His heart gave a mighty lurch. Something had altered in their relationship the past few days, and he wasn't ready to face it. All of her talk about being seen as a lady had made him more aware that she had grown up and was no longer the little girl who used to tag along everywhere he went. He frowned, pushing those thoughts to the back of his mind to consider at a more appropriate time.

"You're early," he told her, noting the anxiety radiating from her violet eyes.

"I wanted to make certain I had all my instructions clear in my head one more time."

Mr. Dailey harrumphed from the doorway of the stage office and they turned his way. His face was shadowed by the light from the office spilling out behind him.

"In that case," he said, "come inside and we'll go over them."

Adam gave the horses' reins to a stable hand and joined Amanda and Mr. Dailey in his office.

Since it was only five o'clock in the morning, much of the city had yet to awaken, but parts of it were already coming to life—the newspaper offices would be hard at work putting out the morning's edition, milkmen would be delivering milk and assorted other businesses would be getting ready for the day. Most streets remained relatively uncluttered, though. That would change in the next couple of hours.

The stage would leave promptly at eight o'clock, with or without its passengers. From experience, Adam knew that at least one person would come hurrying up about five minutes before it was time to leave. Since Mr. Dailey had yet to inform him of those who had purchased tickets, besides the Nightingtons and Mr. Bass, the man who had been in the office the day Amanda had made her incredible request, he had no idea what to expect.

"You are responsible for all of the passengers, packages and, most especially, the mail," Mr. Dailey informed Amanda. His look said that he was already regretting his decision to allow her to conduct. There was a very real possibility the man would lose his job over this despite the ten thousand dollars.

"Whenever a passenger disembarks at a stop, it is up to you to make certain that he is signed for. Since everyone on this trip is traveling through to San Francisco, you will only have to sign them off then."

Adam was surprised. Few people made the through trip, most getting off at points in between, Like Fort Smith in Arkansas. He assumed the lack of passengers getting off early was because of the Nightingtons purchasing the entire stage before more tickets could be bought.

"Do we know anything about the other passengers on this trip?" Adam asked.

"You know about the Nightingtons," Mr. Dailey replied, his set face speaking more loudly than words. He was not particularly happy about the traveling siblings. "Then there is a US marshal returning a prisoner to San Francisco to stand trial for a murder he committed there years ago."

Adam liked the thought of this trip less and less. Had he known about the marshal, he would have done everything in his power to dissuade both Amanda *and* Miss Nightington. He was not happy about this situation. No, he was not happy at all. He met Amanda's look and she gave him a reassuring smile, which fell far short of its intended goal.

"As conductor," Adam told her, "you have the authority to refuse any passengers you think might be detrimental to the trip."

She shook her head and he sighed inwardly. He should have known.

"No. That's fine." She glanced at Mr. Dailey. "Go on, Mr. Dailey."

Adam gritted his teeth. Well, that was fine when she was conducting, but when he took over, it was going to be a different story.

"The mail must never be out of either your or Adam's sight. No matter what happens to anyone or anything else, you are never to lose sight of the mail."

Amanda snapped him a salute, and Adam had to grin at her audacity. A smile quirked the right corner of his mouth only to be eliminated in the next instant when the marshal came in with a manacled prisoner.

The marshal seemed to take in everyone in the room with one encompassing glance. He gave Adam a brief nod, and Adam returned it, studying the two men in return.

The marshal looked like a man who could definitely handle himself. Tall and stocky, his slightly graying hair spoke of a person who knew how to survive his dangerous position.

His prisoner, on the other hand, looked like a man who couldn't care less whether he survived or not. His cocky attitude spoke of a dangerous self-centeredness, one that said he wouldn't hesitate to get someone killed. Adam's eyes narrowed. There was something vaguely familiar about the man, not so much in his looks as in his mannerisms. The way he pushed back his dark hair with a flip of his head pulled at a long-lost memory.

"Sit down," the marshal told his prisoner, shoving him onto the bench beside the door.

Adam didn't like the prisoner's sly smile as it rested on each person in the room. The hate glittering from the man's cold gray eyes sent shivers down Adam's spine and caused the hair to rise on the back of his neck. He made a mental note to ensure his guns were fully loaded, and to help the marshal keep a careful eye on his prisoner.

"Will we be leaving on time?" the marshal asked.

"Eight o'clock sharp." Mr. Dailey nodded. The marshal answered with a grunt and seated himself on the bench next to his prisoner.

Mr. Bass was the next person to arrive. He glanced quickly around the room, his face registering alarm an instant before he pasted on a quick smile when he met Adam's curious look. He squinted at the pendulum clock on the wall through his wire-rimmed glasses, the tension easing from him when he realized it was nearing only seven o'clock. He seated himself on the second bench across from the marshal. Noting the other two men, one in shackles, his eyes widened. He swallowed hard at the deliberately intimidating look the prisoner was giving him and quickly turned away.

Adam decided to skip out now while there was still time, and see about making a few arrangements for the trip, not the least of which was checking both his pistol and rifle. His look caught Amanda's before, giving her a nod, he slipped out the door.

Amanda had no trouble interpreting Adam's last expression. It told her he was regretting his decision to allow her to make this trip, especially now with a criminal aboard. She couldn't blame him; the man made her nervous with his cold, lifeless eyes.

A few minutes after Adam left, the Nightingtons arrived. Amanda took one look and rolled her eyes. *You have got to be kidding!* The brother and sister looked as if they were about to go to a ball instead of board a crowded stagecoach and travel hundreds of miles across a dry, dusty terrain.

The prisoner watched them carefully, his greedy look focused on Evan Nightington's gold cuff links. The marshal noticed his interest and jerked on the manacles that joined them together, giving the man a quelling look. The prisoner glared back at him, sliding down in his seat sulkily. Amanda saw the expression on the prisoner's face and wouldn't give a wooden half disme for the marshal's chances of surviving if the felon ever got loose.

Amanda experienced a moment's unease knowing she was responsible for all of these people. The tension in the room was thick. There was something volatile running beneath everyone's outward calm, putting her and everyone else on edge.

When Adam strode back into the office, her tension eased momentarily until she noticed Rose Nightington's face light up. The primitive feeling that had surged through her earlier now clawed its way through her once again. She firmly stifled the wanton impulses.

"Time to load up," Adam said. "Make certain your luggage is placed beneath your feet."

Rose batted long-fringed eyelashes at him, her mouth forming a small moue. "Really? Is there no way to carry more luggage? This little bag hardly allows me a single change of clothes."

Before he could answer, Evan took her by the arm, giving Adam a warning look. "Forget it. You can buy more when we get to San Francisco."

Amanda was too intent on receiving the mailbag from Mr. Dailey as he removed it from his safe to pay any more attention to the grumbling people.

She reached for the bag, but Dailey did not immediately relinquish it. He grimly clutched one side while she held on to the other, looking at him in question. Slowly, he released it, the expression on his face making it evident he did so with the utmost reluctance.

"Don't worry," she told him softly. "I'll protect it with my life. Like the Good Lord says, 'Trust in the Lord, trust also in me.'"

His chest expanded with a deep breath, his lips pressed grimly together, and releasing the air slowly through his nose, he nodded.

The springs of the Concord coach creaked as each passenger climbed up and took a seat. Normally, there would be nine people inside and a few more sitting on top, but today there were only the five passengers.

The Nightingtons took the more comfortable seat behind the driver's position, and the marshal and his prisoner sat at the rear, where the seats shoved inward against their backs due to the packages in the luggage hold behind them.

That left Mr. Bass to sit singly on the middle seat with nothing but a strap to hang on to for support. He faced the Nightingtons, his knees pressed between their legs.

Amanda was glad she would be sitting with Adam in the driver's seat. She didn't relish the thought of having to be in close proximity to the others, their tension radiating to everyone in their vicinity.

She tossed the mail pouch up to Adam, and then climbed up beside him. Mouth set grimly, his hazel eyes stared into her nervous violet ones for what seemed an eternity before she hastily settled down in the seat. She lifted his rifle and placed it between her knees.

He didn't immediately set out until a cough from Mr. Dailey reminded them of the time. Nodding to the stable hand to release the horses, Adam snapped the whip and the horses instantly sprang into bone-rattling motion.

The morning sunlight was hidden from view behind a thick layer of clouds skirting across the threatening sky. Hardly an auspicious beginning to her first trip. She studied the elements with a practiced eye.

"Looks like rain," she told Adam, and he grunted in agreement. At least the passengers would be somewhat protected if those menacing clouds let loose.

They raced down the streets of Memphis, heading south toward their first stop at the Pike Rail Road. From here to there, the roads were relatively good, but that would change quickly if it rained. As it was, the coach rocked back and forth, up and down, in teeth-jarring convulsions.

Adam studied the darkening sky and must have come to the same conclusion. Picking up the whip, he snapped it forward to miss the rear horses but connect with the lead animals, spurring them on to greater speed. Amanda could hear the squawks and complaints coming from inside the coach as the passengers were thrown around. She and Adam exchanged grins while clinging to their own precarious positions.

The road followed the line of the Mississippi River, and periodically they could hear a steamboat whistle in the distance. The scenery whizzed by in such a blur, Amanda barely had time to make out the ash, cottonwood and sweet gum trees that grew in profusion along the way.

She could see Adam relax with each passing mile. The route was as familiar to him as her own plantation was to her. Whatever his thoughts were, he was keeping them to himself. She decided to carefully feel her way into a conversation, even though the jostling coach and pounding hooves of the straining horses was hardly conducive to a serious discussion.

"How long have you been driving this route?" she yelled over the thundering hooves of the horses.

He glanced over at her briefly, then focused back on the road. "Almost a year," he yelled back.

"Is it true that the Overland Stage Line is in financial trouble?"

He shrugged. "There are rumors."

"What will you do if it goes under?"

He cracked the whip again, and although Amanda didn't see how the horses could go any faster, they did. She clung to the handrail of the coach and her hat at the same time.

"I haven't really thought about it," Adam admitted. The jostling of the coach didn't seem to affect him. He rolled with the stage as though he were part of it. She noticed the way he had his feet planted against the forward rail and positioned herself likewise. It immediately gave her more balance.

And then she asked the question she had wanted an answer to for some time. "Why did you leave, Adam?"

What she really meant was, why did you leave *me*? She thought she had gotten over the past hurt, but bringing up the question now opened up a Pandora's box of feelings she had kept shut away for many years. He looked at her and his face was once again grim.

"Probably for the same reason you did."

Her eyes narrowed. "No one was forcing you to get married that I know of."

Something passed through his eyes that she couldn't interpret. He looked back at the road.

"I wanted to lead my own life," he finally said, and at his closed look, she retreated into silence, deciding this conversation was better left for a time when they didn't have to bellow at each other.

The silence went uninterrupted for many miles until Adam picked up a horn and handed it to her.

"We're close to Madison. Blow the horn to let them know we're coming."

Amanda took the tubed instrument and blew, the sound coming out more a bleat than a trumpet. Adam grinned at her and her face colored hotly.

"Come on, Manny. You've always been full of hot air. Give it a really big blow."

She gave him a look that made him laugh and tried again, this time with more success.

"Good. Now keep it up until we reach the station."

By the time Adam pulled the coach to a wrenching halt, Amanda was nearly blue in the face. She glared at Adam's twitching lips.

She started to get up, but Adam pulled her back down. "Stay put. We'll be here only a few minutes." He leaned over to yell at the occupants of the coach. "Everyone stay inside if you don't want to get left behind."

The groans inside let him know he had been heard. Amanda watched in amazement as the six horses were quickly replaced by six new animals in just a matter of minutes. Standing back, the stable hand lifted an arm for Adam to proceed.

Adam snapped the reins and set the horses in motion once again. He noted Amanda's confused face and chuckled.

"Because we run the horses at full speed, they need to be changed every ten miles or so. Although there are only nineteen main stops for picking up mail and delivering passengers, there are about two hundred and seventy stops all together."

With a dazed look, she shook her head slightly. "I had no idea."

"Well," he declared with trepidation, "I have no idea what it will be like after the first sixty miles. I only know what the other drivers have told me."

"If they can do it, then I know you can," she told him, the confidence in her voice having the same effect it always did. He wanted to live up to her lofty ideals of him, but he was afraid he couldn't. No man could. When you put someone on a pedestal, you were bound to find out that, like everyone else, the person had feet of clay. It had been his main reason for leaving. He could live with sometimes letting other people down, but never Amanda.

"Besides," she reminded him, "you won't be driving all the way."

And why did that not bring him comfort?

"Look," Amanda cried, clutching his sleeve with one hand and pointing with the other.

A doe and her fawn were almost hidden by the trees on their left. The startled creatures hesitated but a moment at the unusual sight of the racing horses and coach, and then quickly bounded into the deeper forest.

From then on, Amanda started looking closer at the passing scenery, leaving him to his thoughts.

It felt good to have her beside him again. He had missed her more than he realized. Leaving had seemed a good idea at the time; now he wasn't so certain.

Why hadn't his parents told him about the Rosses trying to marry off Amanda, and to that no-good, self-opinionated oaf? How could her father even consider such a thing? Adam grew angry again just thinking about it.

He glanced at her now, smiling at the joyful picture she made. At least *she* was content. Unlike most women who fought to keep their bonnets on their head when facing into a rushing wind, Amanda was leaning into it, her hat on the seat beside her.

One side of his mouth tilted wryly. That hair was going to be quite a mess later on. It blew out behind her in cascading chestnut waves, the sunshine giving the strands a warm glow. The freckles across her upturned nose caught his eye, and he remembered her saying they were the bane of her existence. He rather liked them himself.

Laughing in abandon, she turned to face him, her luminous eyes glowing with sheer pleasure. An unusual feeling swept through him, a feeling he shouldn't be having toward his little Amanda. He shoved those feelings aside and gave her a forced smile.

Her look reminded him of his first time driving the stage. It gave one a sense of freedom unlike anything else. Sitting high up on the seat, racing at high speed with the wind blowing in your face, it seemed as though you were flying.

The hovering clouds preceded them and, before they reached Des Arc, they let loose their threatening precipitation. The speed they were traveling made the water droplets feel more like pellets of buckshot.

He handed Amanda a rubber blanket from under the seat and she huddled beneath it, doing her best to protect the mail and rifle.

Adam was thankful to have her out of sight, even if temporarily. He had some thinking to do about these strange thoughts and feelings he was having, and it was better if he could do so without interruption by her.

Chapter 6

Despite the rain, they reached Des Arc with time to spare. While they waited for the horses to be changed, the passengers were invited into Erwin Jackson's station house for a meal.

Adam chose to remain with the mail so Amanda could take the opportunity to eat. She had argued with him about it but, if there was one thing Adam could definitely outdo her in, it was stubbornness.

She watched him from the doorway of the cabin as he oversaw the attaching of the new horses and the loading of the coach onto the ferry to cross the swollen White River.

Although the tea was tepid and watered down, Rose smiled her appreciation at Mrs. Jackson. Amanda had to admit that her first impression of Rose had altered considerably during this trek. The woman was as calm and unruffled by everything going on as though she were out for a congenial buggy ride, despite the fact her earlier pristine appearance had wilted after the past several miles of being thrown around in the traveling coach.

Her brother, on the other hand, sat sulkily in a chair by the fire, trying to dry himself out. Mr. Bass stood next to him, staring unwaveringly into the flickering flames, seemingly as unperturbed and stoical as ever. The man was an enigma. Amanda wasn't quite certain what to make of him.

The marshal and his prisoner were taking advantage of the skimpy meal of bread, fried venison and some as-yet-unrecognizable greens.

Amanda went and sat next to them, curious about their situation. Mrs. Jackson kept a wary eye on the two men as she set another plate of bread on the table.

Amanda thanked her, cutting herself a slice with the razor-sharp knife provided. She noted the prisoner's interest in the implement, and she unobtrusively moved it out of his reach. His lashes lifted slowly until he met her look. The malevolent glitter of his eyes let her know she hadn't been as unobtrusive as she had thought. That dark, "biding my time" look in his eyes sent cold shivers through her.

Amanda tried to ignore him. She turned to the marshal. "Have you been a marshal long, Mr.…?"

"Tucker," he supplied. He nodded, sopping his bread in the venison gravy. His eyes narrowed as he gave her a swift inspection, and she had the decided impression that she wasn't fooling him with her buckskin trappings and hat. "Long enough."

He noticed her quick glances at his prisoner, and he motioned with his shoulder. "I've been tracking Jake here for nigh on two years."

One side of Jake's mouth turned up in a half grin that lacked amusement. Amanda thought it best not to respond. "Are you originally from San Francisco?"

"Naw. I'm from Texas." Tucker finished with his plate

and pushed it aside. Mrs. Jackson came to remove it and he gave her a smile, patting his lean stomach. "Right fine cookin', ma'am."

She seemed surprised by the compliment, and her cheeks colored brightly. Ducking her head in embarrassment, she thanked him and took the empty plate to the washtub in the corner.

The marshal pulled out the fixings for a cigarette and rolled the tobacco while Jake finished his food. Amanda quickly ate her own meal and then hurried outside to watch over the mail so Adam could eat before they were on their way again.

The rain was coming down hard, adding to the already overflowing banks of the river. She met Adam's worried look with one of her own.

"I'll stay here while you get something to eat," she told him.

He shook his head. "I don't want to take the time. We need to get everyone loaded up and across the river before it rises too much higher. You wait here while I get everyone rounded up."

He returned moments later, the others dashing along in his wake and skipping around the largest mud puddles. Amanda opened the door of the stage, and everyone hurriedly boarded to get out of the rain.

Adam motioned to Amanda. "You, too."

She stepped back, frowning at him and shaking her head. "I'm not leaving you up there alone."

"I won't be alone. Dawson here takes over as driver at this point."

Amanda hadn't even noticed the other man standing behind Adam. He glared at her now for holding things up, spurring her into action. She started to climb into the driver's seat, but Adam's hand on hers where it clutched the rail stopped her.

"No," he told her unequivocally.

She wanted to argue with him, but realized he was once again protecting her. Dawson didn't know she was a woman. Besides, as of now Adam was the conductor for the next length of the journey and, as such, he had total authority.

Meeting Adam's serious look, she nodded briefly to show she understood and climbed inside the coach with the others. She found herself crunched between Mr. Bass and several packages that had been tied to the center seat to avoid them being thrown out and lost.

The stage bounced and jostled onto the ferry and then they experienced the undulating motion of the water as they were transported across the river.

"Do you think it's safe?"

Rose's whispered question seemed to be thrown out into the tense silence for anyone to answer.

It was the marshal who replied. "Sure. They've done this plenty of times."

Amanda wasn't so certain. The river was higher than normal from the unexpected amount of rainfall in the area as evidenced by the continuous pounding on the coach's roof.

A sudden jerk sent everyone scrambling for something to hold on to.

The heavy drag from the rushing water caused the pulley rope on the far side of the river to suddenly pull loose from the sodden riverbank. The saturated rope rapidly sank beneath the water while the ferry barge was pushed downstream by the swift current.

"Grab a pole!" Jackson shouted, and Adam left Dawson holding the now-terrified horses while he tried to help the ferryman paddle the boat using the long poles, which were normally used as leverage, by pushing them against the bottom of the river. Each rapid mile they covered by river would mean backtracking several by land to find the already-carved-out overland route.

It required every muscle, and then some, to fight the speeding current. Dawson struggled with the rearing horses and needed his help, but he couldn't stop to give the other man a hand.

The barge dipped and swayed as the horses shifted in terror, water rushing up over the sides and filling Adam's boots. Between that and the pouring rain, he was drenched clear through.

The doubts he had about God no longer seemed significant in the face of such a possible catastrophe. Eight other lives depended on him to keep them safe, and he suddenly realized he wasn't as independent as he had always thought. It was a humbling moment.

"All right, Lord. You've got my attention. Now, please, if you really do care and are listening, get us out of this," he muttered. If anything happened to Amanda, he would never forgive himself. And he was pretty certain there was nowhere on God's green earth he could go where her family wouldn't track him down, especially her uncle.

He felt a presence and, turning his head, found Mr. Bass at his side. Bass grabbed another pole, and with the three of them paddling, they were able to more quickly cover the extra distance to the far side of the river. The flat bottom touched the shore, and Jackson hurried to attach a line.

Before he could get the ferry secure, the terrified horses pulled from Dawson's grasp and crashed through the wooden-fence barricade surrounding the four sides of the craft, and charged up the bank on the other side.

Adam dropped his pole and ran after them, Dawson close on his heels. Thankfully the muddy bank slowed the horses enough for Adam to grasp the back side of the carriage just as they gained a more secure footing and galloped off for the distant forest.

If he didn't get them stopped in time...

His wet fingers were sliding off the leather straps that latched together the rear backing of the coach.

Amanda peered out the window of the stage, saw Adam clinging like a limpet to the back and Dawson running along behind. She sucked in a horrified breath. Just as she took in the implication of what she was seeing, Adam's grip slipped and he slid to the ground, his dismayed eyes meeting hers as the horses continued to run.

The horses were gaining speed. Amanda looked ahead and saw the tree line fast approaching. If the horses reached the forest, the coach would be torn apart by the trees. She leaned out, frozen in indecision. The responsibility for the five lives in this coach was hers and Adam's; she had to do something, and do it fast. But what?

"What's goin' on?" the marshal yelled, clinging to the overhead leather handhold.

Amanda glanced back at him, schooling her expression to hide her fear. There was only one thing she could think to do. Mustering her courage, she yelled at the marshal, "Nothing. Just hang on."

Grabbing the lip of the door, she pulled herself out the window until she was sitting with her legs dangling inside the coach.

"Are you out of your mind? Get back in here!"

Ignoring Evan's command, she reached up and found a hold, pulling herself up until her feet rested on the window ledge. The rain blinded her for a few seconds. Blinking rapidly to clear her vision, she saw the tree line getting closer. The coach hit a bump and she lost her footing, clinging to the top of the stage while her legs bounced against the side of the carriage. Rose screamed.

Amanda scrambled hand over hand sideways until she finally managed to pull herself up onto the driver's seat. A feeling of déjà vu overcame her as she was transfixed at the sight of the six large horses and the blurring ground racing beneath their flying hooves. But unlike that time on the plantation, thankfully, Adam had tied the reins securely to the top rail and she wouldn't have to jump between the moving horses to pick them up. She loosened the reins and pulled with all her might, but her strength was no match for the panicked horses.

She struggled to pull the brake while still holding the reins. Although the brake slowed the team, they were still too close to the trees. Amanda could think of only one thing to do. If she couldn't stop them, she would just have to turn them.

Wrapping the reins around her waist, she leaned her body hard to put enough pressure on the lead horses' bits to cant their heads to the right. Although they fought the bit, they finally turned. Amanda kept leaning until the horses were pulled into a half circle, heading back the way they had come.

Turning slowed them enough so that when they crossed paths with Adam, he was able to jump forward and latch on to the reins. Amanda sucked in a breath as she saw him pulled between the racing team, but they finally slowed and then came to a full stop.

The horses shuddered, blowing out heavy breaths, while Amanda practically sank onto the seat, her body quivering with delayed reaction.

"Adam!" she screamed.

His head appeared between the lead horses as he stood, and Amanda closed her eyes, releasing her pent-up breath. She quickly scrambled from the coach and ran to him, throwing herself into his arms. They closed around her tightly, nearly squeezing the breath from her lungs.

"Are you all right?" they asked in unison.

Amanda gave a nervous chuckle, but looking up at Adam, she could tell by his face he found absolutely nothing to be amused about.

"Are you sure you're all right?" he asked again, pushing back the hair from her face with shaking fingers.

"Fine," she told him, her heart only now slowing its frantic rhythm. "And you?"

"A few cuts and bruises. Other than that, I'll do."

Dawson reached them at the same time Evan Nightington tumbled out of the coach. Dawson handed Adam his hat, his appreciative look settling on Amanda.

"Well, don't you beat all?" he drawled. "Who would have ever thought a little half-pint like you was capable of such a rescue?"

"Miss Ross, are you all right?" Evan asked, his eyes raking over her for any signs of injury.

Dawson's startled look flew back to her. "Miss?"

His face changed from approbation to fury in an instant, and Amanda sighed, knowing what was about to come. Before he could say anything, Adam intervened.

"Dailey knows, and we don't have time to argue about it. We need to get back to the route and get this stage back on track."

The look Adam gave Dawson made the other man press his lips tightly together. Slapping his hat against his thigh to release frustration, he strode over and pulled himself up to the driver's seat.

Amanda looked from one to the other. There was history between these two men, something she would like to find out from Adam when they had time.

He turned to her, his eyes raking over her in the same manner as Evan's had earlier. "Are you sure you're all right?"

She noticed the marshal, Jake and Rose peering from

the window in varying degrees of awe and respect. Embarrassed, she gave Adam a halfhearted smile.

"I'm fine. Let's get going." She glanced quickly around. "Where's Mr. Bass?"

Adam pointed to the river in the distance where Mr. Bass was standing with Mr. Jackson beside the newly tethered ferry watching them.

Now that the excitement was over, Amanda was feeling the effects of the rapid release of adrenaline to her system. She lethargically climbed back into the stagecoach on shaking legs, thankful the whole affair had ended well. She sank onto the hard seat, grateful she didn't have to be the conductor for the next leg of the journey.

Evan followed her inside, seating himself by his sister across from Amanda. His mouth tilted upward on one side.

"I think I owe you an apology."

Amanda's brows winged in surprise. "Whatever for?"

"For the uncharitable thoughts I had about you," he replied, and then settled back against the seat without further comment. Rose dipped her head in concurrence, the look of respect in her eyes one Amanda wouldn't soon forget.

Quiet reigned as they started to move. They stopped long enough to pick up Mr. Bass. He gave Amanda a look that was hard to interpret before settling into the seat beside her.

If the road was bumpy previously, crossing unbroken land near the river was a nightmare. Before they finally reached the overland route, everyone's hands were raw from gripping the leather handholds.

Adam saw Dawson shake his head and knew what was coming before the man said anything.

"A woman! What was Dailey thinking?"

Since the rain had finally ceased, Adam pulled the logbook from under the seat, noting the incident at the river.

"You know Taylor Ross?" Adam asked without looking up.

Dawson glanced at him, frowning. "Yeah, I know Taylor. What's he got to do with anything?"

"Manny is his niece."

Dawson's jaw dropped. "Well, don't that beat all! That little pint-size thing?"

Adam grinned at him. "Don't let her size fool you. That little pint-size thing, as you call her, is like a little bundle of dynamite."

At Dawson's skeptical look, Adam laughed outright. He would see. They all would before this trip was over.

The smile left his face. Hopefully, there wouldn't be any more such incidents. He didn't think his heart could handle it. The picture of Amanda climbing out the stage window and over the side like a little spider still had his blood rushing through him faster than the White River they had just crossed.

He was only beginning to realize just how much he had missed her and her hoydenish ways. Dawson interrupted his thoughts.

"We're really behind schedule. We're gonna have to make up some time."

A look passed between them, and Adam nodded grimly.

Dawson picked up the whip, cracking it with expert ease and sending the horses pitching forward at a faster pace. It was dangerous to be going at such high speeds on roads wet from heavy rains, but they would just have to take their chances.

Darkness was already beginning to fall when they reached the next relay point. Adam sounded out the horn until they skidded to a halt in front of a rough dwelling housing the Overland agent.

The horses were quickly changed and a rider with a lantern joined the group to lead the way through the encroaching darkness. Adam had never been on a night ride before but, like the other drivers, he would feel comfortable doing so on his own route; he knew it that well. He had faith in Dawson; it was the condition of the roads that worried him.

They took off again, the lantern barely lighting the way. Still, they knew the rider would signal if there was a real problem.

The farther west they traveled, the drier the roads became, as little rain had fallen in this area in the past few days.

The moon was three-quarters full and bright, adding to the lantern light. Dark shadows in the surrounding forests gave an eerie impression of figures skulking among the trees.

Although the Indians on this part of the trail were relatively friendly, there was the occasional band of renegades. Adam tightened his grip on his rifle and searched the surrounding forests carefully.

Night turned into day and on they traveled. By now, the passengers had become inured to the constant motion of the bouncing coach and the short stops only briefly allowing them to relieve themselves.

They finally rolled into Fort Smith three hours ahead of time because each driver had pushed the horses to their fullest extent. From here, Adam had no idea what the future trail would entail.

Chapter 7

Amanda stood on the street in front of the hotel at Fort Smith on quivering legs. There wasn't much to see in the darkness, but even at midnight, the saloon was in full swing, its light and noise spilling into the dark farther down the street.

The passengers took the opportunity to make use of the hotel's amenities while Amanda handed over the mail to the agent for this stop, picked up the mail for Saint Louis that would be traveling on, and examined the waybills.

Adam had disappeared, and she felt a moment's panic, quickly squelched when she reminded herself that he would never desert her.

He had introduced her to the new driver, a Mr. Collins, without mentioning that she was a woman. The other man had merely given her a brief inspection before nodding and helping Adam switch the stage for the sturdier celerity wagon and the team of horses for the mules that would be used for the rest of the trip. If he found the situation of permanent conductors unusual, he kept his thoughts to himself.

Now the driver was rounding up the passengers, and Adam still hadn't returned. Amanda glanced around apprehensively, sighing with relief when she saw him striding out of the darkness.

After helping the driver hand the other passengers into the new stage, Adam pulled her to a stop when she would have climbed in after them.

"I telegraphed your father," he told her, and she froze, her wide eyes meeting his.

"They needed to know, Manny," he told her softly. "They're probably worried sick about you right now."

She shook her head. "No. They would think I was still with Aunt Lucinda."

His mouth twisted. "Are you really that naive? Your father would have contacted your aunt long before now to see how you're doing. You've never been able to take two steps without him being there to check on you."

Amanda suddenly felt guilty at her self-centeredness. She looked into Adam's dearly loved face and remembered just how she had felt when he had disappeared from their lives. Even when he had finally contacted them, she had continued to worry about him, her thoughts with him day and night.

"What did you tell them?"

He placed his hands on her shoulders and squeezed reassuringly. "I told them you had decided to take a trip on the Overland stage to San Francisco and that I would be with you to see that you are taken care of."

She sighed heavily. Now Adam had been drawn into her subterfuge, and her father was not a very forgiving man. "I'm sorry."

He smiled. "Don't worry about it. Let's just cross one river at a time."

Her lips tilted wryly at his double entendre. After the number of streams and rivers they had already crossed, the rest should be a piece of cake.

Unlike the Concord stage, the celerity wagon had no hard roof, but rather a canvas top. No one could sit on top, nor could the mail, so everything had to be stuffed inside with the passengers, making the coach even more crowded.

The wagon was open sided, the canvas coverings rolled up to allow the embarking passengers admittance. Amanda didn't think very highly of the less solid stage, especially knowing they were about to cross into some of the most rugged terrain in the territory, but they had already been shown to withstand the rigors of the trail, so she decided to relax and let the driver do the worrying. She had enough worries of her own.

The wagon dipped as Collins and Adam climbed into the front driver's seat. Unlike the Concord stage, the driver's seat on the celerity wagon was level with the passenger seating. Just having Adam that little bit closer, and hearing his deep voice so near, eased Amanda's tension.

"Hang on," the driver shouted, warning them they were about to begin. The coach jerked forward at the cracking of the whip, and they were once again on their way.

After four days of travel, it didn't take them long to acclimatize to the new coach's jolting and jarring.

Amanda looked up and found Evan's appraising eyes fixed on her. His sister, too, stared at her in what appeared to be amazed fascination. Amanda shifted her shoulders nervously, looking away to the blurring darkness outside the racing wagon.

She glanced back and found them still watching her. She grew irritated under their steady regard.

"Is there a problem?" she asked irritably.

Rose started and then quickly turned her inspection elsewhere. Not so her brother.

"Are there many women like you in this country?" he asked, to be interrupted by his sister's, "Evan!"

"I apologize for my brother's rudeness," she hurried to say. She glared at him a moment before smiling at Amanda. "Everything is so different here. We're having a hard time…adjusting."

Amanda shrugged, unaccountably hurt. Hadn't she been trying to shed the image of the prim and proper miss she had been brought up to be? So why, when faced with this beautiful picture of modesty and decorum, was she suddenly upset?

"There's no need to apologize," she told them, choosing to look at Evan instead of his sister. "But to answer your question, I have no idea if there are others who dress like me. I'm assuming that's what you meant?" She lifted a brow in inquiry.

He blinked several times before answering. "I…uh… yes. Yes, that's what I was referring to."

Amanda chose to allow the falsehood to pass. Rose changed the subject.

"So where are you from?" she inquired. "Not that I am very familiar with the United States."

"I'm from Tennessee. Outside Nashville to be exact. My father owns a plantation there."

Evan's dark look settled on her. "I suppose he owns slaves?"

"Evan!" Rose interrupted again. "Mind your manners!"

She gave him a warning glare that caused him to subside into his seat sulkily, which abruptly ended any further conversation. Amanda chose not to answer his question. It was a tricky subject in this country and one that was causing a rift she didn't think could be solved by diplomacy.

Adam heard the conversation between the Nightingtons and Amanda. He could have easily answered the first question. No, there wasn't another woman like Amanda in the whole world, much less this country. She was unique. One of a kind.

Something about the way Nightington had asked the question had put his teeth on edge. There was just that hint of...what was the word he was looking for? *Admiration?*

As for the second question, it would do Nightington well to remember that it hadn't been all that long since England not only owned slaves, but transported them for sale in other places, as well.

Not that he could blame the man for his seeming anger at the injustice of slavery. Although Adam had been raised around such beliefs himself for most of his life, it hadn't been until his later years that he had given it much thought one way or another.

The plight of the slaves had been brought to his attention when his father had tried to force him into a junior version of himself. But for years, he had wanted to strike out on his own and be like Amanda's uncle, free to live life without all the strict conventions of the time. Free to traipse across this as-yet-unexplored country and maybe even find the God that Uncle Taylor had found in the wild hills and valleys of this land.

That God was a far cry from the one he had heard preached on his father's plantation, which stressed that slaves were to obey their masters. The God of Uncle Taylor believed that all men were created equal.

"We're coming up on the river."

Collins interrupted his thoughts, bringing them to a screeching halt.

"Macy will light the way with the lantern, but keep a sharp eye out for quicksand. The water level here is higher than normal, so it's hard to see where the deep sand is."

Macy was the Butterfield agent whose job it was to lead the wagon with a lantern while it was still dark. The Arkansas River was running higher due to the recent rains, and she was hiding her secret sandpits well.

Instead of a ferry, this time they would merely ford the river. The mules began to hesitate, reluctant to enter the swift-moving water. Collins cracked the whip, spurring them on.

They plunged down the steep bank and into the churning water. Bouncing and jolting, they arrived at the other side without mishap, and the mules staggered their way up the even steeper bank on the other side.

They picked up their pace and were hurrying through the early-morning darkness once again. Collins said nothing until they were close to the next station and he reminded Adam to blow the horn.

"We're in Indian Territory now," he told Adam. "The Choctaw are safe enough. It won't get tricky until we reach Comanche territory on the far west side."

They were seventeen miles from the river. The next station was the home of Governor Walker, a man who was said to have Choctaw blood running through his veins.

Adam was surprised when the governor's house eventually came into view. Unlike the many dilapidated log huts they had passed along the road, Governor Walker's house was large and well built.

The governor himself came out to help hitch up fresh mules.

Amanda climbed down from the wagon and joined Adam.

"It's my turn to take watch," she told him, bending and stretching to get the kinks out of her back and legs.

He didn't bother to argue with her. Truth to tell, he was beginning to feel the need of a little sleep, and it would be easier to get it sitting inside.

Dawn was beginning to lighten the sky, and the area around stirred to life. It was easier to see the magnitude of the Walker farm, its acreage stretching for as far as the eye could see. Several hundred head of cattle were grazing in the fields beyond, dark-skinned slaves keeping watch over them.

Rose climbed down from the stage and stood beside Adam and Amanda. Her eyes narrowed as she studied the slaves watching over the cattle and caring for the crops.

"Are slaves allowed in Indian Territory?"

Adam shrugged. "Slavery has been a big part of the Indian life since before the white man came. The difference now is they purchase slaves instead of taking them by force."

Adam glanced at her and saw her lips thin, her face settling into an unattractive scowl. She caught his look and her face was suddenly transformed by a playful smile.

"Did I hear Miss Ross say you would be joining us inside for the next few miles?" she asked, adroitly changing the subject.

He hoped the woman didn't plan on his being sociable, because he really did need to get some sleep. He had been awake for almost forty-eight hours.

The look on Amanda's face surprised him. She was practically scowling at Rose. He could only wonder at what had happened to put that expression on Amanda's normally congenial face.

"Yes, I am. I need to get some sleep."

He hoped she would take the hint. He was man enough to be flattered by her attempts at flirtation, but there was a time and a place, and the untamed wilds of the United States territories wasn't it.

When he joined them in the coach, it was fairly obvious she hadn't taken his earlier hint. She seated herself across from him and started a rambling conversation that, despite his best efforts to be a proper gentleman, eventually put him to sleep.

* * *

Amanda breathed in the fresh, invigorating air. Because they had spent several days in the same clothing and had not been able to bathe, the inside of the coach reeked of human sweat. The cologne that Rose used to try to cover the strong scent only made it worse. After several hours, Amanda had a pounding headache.

She was beginning to be bothered by the other woman's attempts to get Adam's attention, although why it should irritate her so much was still a mystery.

Maybe it was because even after several days, Rose, despite being somewhat bedraggled, was as beautiful as ever. She was a woman both her parents and Adam's would approve of—the picture of elegant society.

And what about Adam? Was Rose the kind of woman to win his heart? The thought left Amanda feeling unaccountably depressed.

The trees began to thin the farther they traveled. Amanda began to count each stop they made as being one less before they reached their destination. After several days, she realized that making this trip was not something she would like to continue as a career. The tedious monotony, the cramped conditions, the poor food the farther they got from civilization, all contributed to the growing irritation among the travelers, herself included. She almost wished something exciting would happen to relieve the monotony.

Just shy of Blackburn's station, they passed from the small plains to a densely forested area where the road was rougher than anything they had experienced so far. Amanda had to cling to the seat with both hands to keep from being thrown from the coach.

Behind her, she could hear the protests of the passengers as they tried to maintain some kind of handhold to keep from being thrown around inside.

"Don't you think we should slow down?" she yelled to the driver. He was unfamiliar to her, having taken up driving at the last station. He only grinned, cracking the whip to spur the mules to greater speed.

They hit a particularly large rock that bounced one of the wagon's wheels high into the air and almost cata-pulted Amanda from her seat. If she hadn't been hanging on tightly, she would be picking herself up from the road right now.

The wagon came down hard and Amanda heard a loud crack. The carriage tilted, almost overturning. Yells and screams coming from inside the coach assured her the passengers were having no better time of it than she was.

A wheel came off the back right side, causing the wagon to lurch sideways and skid on the ground. The mules, feel-ing the weight of the wagon pulling against them, reared and fought the traces, stopping the coach in the middle of the road.

Amanda glared at the now-repentant driver as he fought to keep control of the animals. She jumped from the seat and ran to the front and, grabbing the bridle of the lead mule, tried to calm him as he fought against her. But her size was no match for the now-panicked animal.

Adam joined her, snatching the bridle of the second lead mule. He fought the rearing animal, his powerful arm muscles bunching against the leather sleeves of his jacket.

The mule's hoof caught Amanda upside the head, send-ing her hat flying, and she staggered backward, disori-ented for a moment. She heard Adam yelling but couldn't make out the words as the scene before her faded in and out while bright flashes of light danced before her eyes.

She felt someone grab her and thrust her to a sitting position on the ground, pushing her head down between her upraised knees.

Barely cognizant of the sounds around her, it was some time before she realized the pandemonium had stilled. When she finally lifted her swimming head, it was to find Mr. Bass kneeling next to her. He was using one of the water canteens to wet a handkerchief, which he then used to swipe at the blood trickling unheeded down her cheek.

"Miss Ross, can you hear me?" he asked, and for the first time she noticed the color of his eyes behind the wire-rimmed glasses. The brown orbs were full of concern.

She nodded and then groaned at the pain it caused.

Adam skidded to his knees on the ground in front of her. "Manny! Manny, are you all right?"

He pushed Mr. Bass aside, sitting on the ground next to her and taking her into his arms. Lifting her chin, he quickly surveyed the damage, pressing back the hair from her face with gentle fingers.

She pushed at his hands. "The mail. Stay with the mail."

"Hang the mail!" he ground out. "The driver can watch it. I'm more concerned about you."

"I'm fine," she told him, trying to get to her feet. "And I wouldn't trust that crazy driver with anything!" she practically shouted. "Thank the Good Lord that he takes care of the simpleminded as well as the righteous." The look she threw the driver left no one in any doubt as to whom she meant.

Adam wrapped his arm around her waist, helping her to stand. His face was so white she thought he might be the one to faint. The thought brought a slight smile to her face.

"I don't know what you think is so funny!" he snarled. Realizing the extent of his concern, she laid a hand against his cheek to ease his tension. After several days of growth, the whiskers on his face tickled her fingers. She softly stroked his cheek, amazed at the rough, yet at the same time, silky texture.

Her look met his and held. Her searching gaze tried to find the reason for her sudden lack of breath in the depths of his eyes, their normally hazel color hidden by the intense blackness of his pupils.

She could feel the thunder of his heart beneath her hand resting on his chest and realized her own pounded just as furiously and, unlike his, hers raced not from fear. For one brief moment, it seemed as though their hearts beat as one.

Confused, she pushed out of his hold and stepped away. Macy, the man who rode horseback and carried the lantern, joined them, breaking the tense mood.

"The axle's broken," he told them. "I need to ride on to Blackburn station and get a new coach and bring it back."

Adam sighed. "Putting us further behind."

Macy shrugged. "Can't be helped."

"It could have been!" Amanda argued, throwing the driver another disgusted glare. She struggled to control her irritation. What was done was done, and her anger wouldn't help matters any.

Adam helped Macy unhook the mules from the wagon where he would then take them to Blackburn's and return with a new team and, hopefully, a new coach. Macy remounted his horse and, with the mules in tow, disappeared into the darkness.

"You mean we're stuck here?"

Amanda turned at Evan's voice. "Just for a while," she assured him.

At his concerned look, Adam said, "You needn't worry about getting to San Francisco on time. The stage has been making the trip four days earlier than the schedule. Barring unforeseen circumstances, we should still make it in timely fashion."

Adam glanced briefly at Amanda and quickly returned

to the stage. She frowned after him, still trying to figure out exactly what had happened between them.

She studied the now-tilted coach, remembering her earlier thoughts. Never again would she test Providence by wishing for something to break the monotony.

Chapter 8

Using dry wood from the surrounding forest, Adam quickly prepared a fire to stave off the cold temperatures, which were steadily dropping as the sun began to set in a glorious display of vivid red, orange and purple.

It would be several hours before Macy would return with another coach. In the meantime, they could take the opportunity of the unexpected delay to get some much-needed rest.

Outside the confines of the stage, the cold would be more apparent, yet none of the passengers seemed inclined to reenter the tilted vehicle despite the fact the canvas drapes would lessen the effects of the wind. The chill February zephyr was lessened by the surrounding forest, but as the darkness increased, so would the effects of the dropping temperatures.

Adam made a note of the accident in the logbook, glancing up when he heard raised voices.

The fringe on Amanda's buckskin jacket was flying

about violently as she gesticulated at the driver, her face etched with ire, and puffs of frost forming with each blistering mouthful. Hollis stood resolute before her, hands planted firmly on his hips, his dark countenance warning of an imminent explosion. The passengers were standing nearby, witnessing the tense exchange. *What was that all about?*

He strode over and interrupted their heated conversation.

"What's going on here?"

Amanda turned blazing plum-colored eyes to his. "I was just telling Mr. Hollis here that he will *not* be driving the rest of the trip to Blackburn station."

"And I was telling this young whippersnapper that he can't tell me what to do!"

Adam's narrow-eyed gaze settled on the man, and Hollis's face changed from anger to wariness at Adam's look. "Actually, *she* can," he told the man, stressing the feminine gender. "She is the conductor, and as conductor, she has complete authority over you."

The man stared at Amanda in surprise, his look going slowly from the top of her head to the toes of her moccasins.

"She?" he asked in amazement.

Hollis stood openmouthed, not knowing how to respond. His brows beetled downward, and he glared at Amanda.

"I ain't takin' no orders from a woman!"

Adam was about to step in when he caught Amanda's warning look. She was right. If he interceded it would just diminish her authority. He tensed as Amanda stepped forward to stand toe-to-toe with the driver. Although Amanda was fairly short, Hollis wasn't much taller, but he was from that rough-and-ready breed known as a frontiersman. The Butterfield chose men like these because of their ability to survive in harsh conditions, and they were not a type of man to be messed with. Amanda and Hollis glared into each other's eyes.

"Then you are fired," she told him, her voice laced with steel.

His eyes widened. "You cain't fire me!"

"Actually, she can," Adam disagreed. "The conductor is responsible for the stage and its occupants. If he, or *she*, feels you are a danger to either, she has the authority to fire you." His look let the man know that although he didn't say anything, he was there to back her up.

"If I were you, sir," Evan interrupted, "I wouldn't argue with the lady."

The admiration in the man's voice made Adam grit his teeth in silent protest, and he pinned Evan with a narrow-eyed look. The man retreated two steps.

Hollis frowned at Evan. "Well, you ain't me, and *she* ain't no lady!"

Amanda glanced at Adam, and he couldn't miss the wounded look that passed through her eyes. "Make a note in the logbook that due to irresponsible actions that endangered the coach and those within," she said, "Mr. Hollis has been fired."

Adam had no idea what had transpired while Amanda was with the driver, but as she wasn't a vindictive person, it must have been serious, and he wasn't about to doubt her. He made the note, daring Hollis with a look to cause any further trouble.

Hollis slammed his hat on his head. "I'll appeal to the superintendent!" He stormed off to sit beside the fire.

He could see Amanda let out a slow breath, and he gave her a sympathetic smile.

"Well, I don't know about the rest of you," the marshal interjected, interrupting the tense atmosphere, "but while I'm not being thrown about all over the place, I'm going to catch some shut-eye."

Adam agreed. His mind was almost numb with exhaustion. The other passengers grumblingly agreed, and everyone found a spot close to the fire to at least rest while waiting for the stage.

Amanda kneeled beside Adam. She studied his face. "You look tired," she said softly.

With a finger, he traced a path across the dark circles under her eyes that told their own story. "As do you," he returned just as softly. What had he been thinking? Regardless of her strength and resilience, Amanda was still a genteel lady no matter how much she would like someone to think otherwise. Her father would have every right to call him out when they got back. *If* they got back. He never should have agreed to this trip, but what was done, was done. They had come too far to turn back now.

"Get some sleep, Adam," she told him, the breathy catch in her voice at his touch causing his own breathing to react in an odd way. "I'll keep watch and tend the fire."

He started to shake his head, but she reached up and placed a hand on each side of his face, moving his head up and down. She had removed her leather gloves, and her fingers were warm against his chilled jaw.

"Say, yes, Amanda. Thank you, Amanda."

He grinned at her, the smile slowly fading from his face as they continued to study each other. The pupils of her eyes darkened with reaction to his intense stare. He sucked in a breath, the confusion on her face mirroring what he was feeling at his reaction to her touch. For a moment, he forgot what they had been discussing. Mentally shaking himself, he was surprised at the huskiness of his voice when he said, "Only if you agree to let me take the next two relays."

She dropped her hands to her sides and stepped back, a frown drawing down her dark brows. "That's two hundred and forty miles, Adam. That's too long."

"A little over twenty-four hours," he argued softly. "Trust me to know my limits, Manny."

He could see the arguments forming in her eyes, but she eventually sighed in resignation. "I trust you," she said finally, and giving him one last look, went to join the others by the fire.

Since everyone else was huddled close to the flames, he climbed into the teetering coach, folded down the bench backs and spread himself out. As he was about to drift off, his thoughts wandered into paths he had been trying hard not to follow.

Holding Amanda in his arms earlier, feeling her thundering heart beating against his, had caused his body to react in a decidedly unbrotherly-like way. And just now. What on earth had happened in those few brief minutes? He felt as if he had been turned inside out, upside down and round and round, much like the time he had tried to break his father's prize stallion.

Amanda's trembling lips had practically begged to be kissed, and he realized he wanted to be the man who did so. He frowned, trying hard to push those thoughts aside, but, like a broken dam, he had a feeling that once loosened, the flood of his emotions could never be forced back behind those walls again.

This was Amanda he was talking about, for goodness' sake. She had always been like a little sister to him. Even now, her eyes looked at him with absolute confidence. He would rather cut off his right arm than betray that trust. Feeling as if he was committing some sort of sin, he ground his teeth and, once again, forced those thoughts to the back of his mind. Thankfully, exhaustion overcame him before his thoughts could betray him any more.

Amanda stirred the fire and added more of the dead wood that Adam had collected. The crackling and popping, along with the soughing of the wind through the trees, created a peaceful feeling, which was unfortunately disrupted by Hollis, who sat across from her glaring his bottled-up rage. She shivered, and not just from the cold. From the vindictive look in his eyes, both he and the prisoner seemed to have been cut from the same kind of cloth.

Everyone else seemed to be sleeping, though how they could do so in the below-freezing temperature was beyond her. Wrapped in a blanket, Rose huddled next to her brother while the marshal, handcuffed to his sleeping prisoner, was sawing logs in his sleep. She could hardly blame them. It was almost impossible to get any sleep when you had to sit up all the time and, for those seated near the open doorways, to keep your feet from dropping outside and getting caught in the wheels.

She got up to go check on Adam. Even before she reached the coach, she could hear his gentle snoring. Her lips curved into a soft smile. The poor man was exhausted. So was she, for that matter, but she had been able to catnap more often than he had. Rose had made sure of that.

She frowned. The other woman took every opportunity to talk to Adam, sitting as close to him as she could possibly get. Amanda had to give Adam credit. He never encouraged her. Nevertheless, Rose was like a hound on the scent, with Adam as her prey.

Amanda recognized her feelings for what they were: pure, unmitigated jealousy and possessiveness.

Was it possible her feelings for Adam were evolving, or had she always felt this way about him and just never admitted it to herself? When he had held her in his arms, the feelings that had rushed through her had not been like those of years past. These new feelings were more intense, more profound, and she didn't know what to do about them.

The mere touch of his finger had set her to trembling, making her breathing falter.

Adam would be so embarrassed if he knew. She had pulled away from him before she could make a fool of herself by throwing herself into his arms. If she ever did anything to hurt their friendship, she would find it unforgivable.

She must keep him from suspecting anything. But how was she going to accomplish that sitting next to him mile after mile? She thought about returning to the coach when he took his turn sitting next to the driver as conductor, but that thought held little appeal.

She returned to her spot near the fire and noted that Hollis had drifted off to sleep. Being free from his baleful glare, her nerves finally calmed.

The sun had gone down behind the horizon a long time ago and the air was growing chillier by the minute. She huddled closer to the fire and let her thoughts wander.

What had her father thought when he received Adam's telegraph? In truth, she had given very little thought to how her parents would react to her being gone. Adam was right. She was a selfish, spoiled little girl. When she returned home, she would apologize and hope that she could make her father understand she was no longer a child.

She knew her parents loved her, but it was a suffocating kind of love. She hated to cause them worry, though she hoped by using this bid for independence, she could show them she was stronger than they gave her credit for. Somehow, she didn't think her father was going to see it that way. He would probably lock her up until Judgment Day, or until it was time for her arranged marriage, whichever came first.

Stars appeared in the night sky one by one until the inky darkness was filled with glowing spheres.

Amanda picked out the Big Dipper and thought about the stories she had heard of slaves following that celestial gourd to freedom in the North. Some of her father's slaves had disappeared, as well. She hoped they had found a better life in the North. She couldn't blame them for wanting to be free and independent; it was very much how she felt herself.

This conflict of beliefs between her father and her over the issue of slavery was one of the things that had set her on her current path. It was getting harder to bear the sight of those individuals trodden by the burden of slavery. Not that her father allowed his slaves to be abused. He would be considered by many to be too lenient. If given the chance, she knew many of the slaves on her father's plantation would choose to stay, but there were others with a hunger for freedom in their eyes. She understood that hunger all too well.

If her uncle had given her the yearning to explore, her Aunt Lucinda had, in the short time they had spent together over the years, instilled in Amanda her abolitionist ideas. It had surprised Amanda that her father had agreed to let her stay with Aunt Lucinda in Memphis, knowing her anti-slavery stance. Still, Aunt Lucinda had always been mother's favorite sister and, despite her views, was still held in high esteem by her father.

Which brought her thoughts full circle to the deception she had played against her parents.

Forgive me, Lord, for my deceit and my selfish ways. When I get back, I will apologize and ask forgiveness. Please be with me and allow me that opportunity.

And what about Adam?

She was beginning to seriously doubt her motives for wanting this job. She claimed she wanted to prove that she could take care of herself, but was that so? How could she stand on her own two feet if she ran to Adam at the first opportunity she got?

Adam had always been her anchor in a turbulent sea. He was always the one she ran to when her world turned upside down, and it couldn't be more upside down than at the moment.

And what had happened to the young, laughing boy who had always taken her to church on Sundays? What had happened to his faith that he couldn't even ask a simple blessing on the food anymore?

She jumped when Adam dropped down beside her. Folding his arms around his upturned knees, he gave her a sideways glance.

"What are you thinking about so hard?"

She ignored his question. "You didn't sleep very long."

"Long enough," he rebutted. "Macy should be back with the wagon soon." He turned his attention to the fire, throwing on some extra wood, then glanced back at her. "You didn't answer my question."

She was reluctant to make her thoughts known to him, and it bothered her that this was so. There was a restraint between them that hadn't been there before, and she wasn't certain what to do to put them back on their earlier footing. Or even if she could, for that matter.

At her hesitation, he said, "You can still talk to me, Manny. If you're in trouble, I want to help."

She smiled. Typical Adam. Always rushing to her rescue.

"Actually, I was thinking about you."

His face registered his surprise. "What about me?" he asked cautiously.

To keep from looking at him, she picked up a small stick and began snapping it into pieces that she threw into the fire.

"You've changed, Adam."

He didn't deny it. "I've grown up, Manny."

She met his look, and their eyes held. "Does growing up mean turning your back on God?"

His brow grew troubled, and he looked away. "I haven't

turned my back on Him. I just think if there is a God, He doesn't really have time to worry about the likes of me." His voice lowered to a near whisper. "Or anyone else for that matter."

Something must have happened to him to put that disillusioned look on his face; something terrible. Perhaps it had been when he seemed to have disappeared off the face of the earth for almost two years. There had been no contact from him whatsoever, and then a year ago, a letter had arrived telling her about working for the Butterfield. And perhaps that was why she was here now. She had just about gone insane with worry when no one had heard from him, not even his family. Again, she questioned her motives for being here. Was it to prove something to herself, or to find Adam?

When she had seen him in Mr. Dailey's office, her heart had almost flown out of her chest. He was alive, even though there was a hardness in his eyes that hadn't been there before. It had brought her up short when she would have thrown herself into his arms.

"He cares," she rebuked him softly. "And so do I."

He met her look, staring at her for several long seconds. His eyes slowly darkened with whatever thoughts were running through his mind, and he suddenly focused on her lips. Something about that look made her insides turn into a puddle of mush. Her breath caught in her throat and her lips parted in unconscious invitation. His eyes flew back to hers. Whatever he saw there made him quickly turn away to stare into the fire once again.

Adam sucked in air, trying to still his volatile emotions. He had to will himself to breathe normally.

It would seem he had changed even more than he thought. Especially where Amanda was concerned. Those eyes. Those lips. He brushed his hands through his hair, pushing his palms against his temples to try to stop the flood of mental images flowing through his mind with the strength of a riptide.

Memories he had ruthlessly locked away were struggling to free themselves with Amanda's innocuous questions.

"What happened, Adam?"

Her soft, melodious voice soothed the raging tide inside him. He had kept things locked up inside for too long, eating away at him like a cancer. Maybe it was time to tell someone, and he could think of no one he could trust more. But would it change her opinion of him? She had always considered him her knight in shining armor. What would she say if she found out just how tarnished that armor had become?

Dropping his hands to his upraised knees, he peered up at the night sky, his mouth set in a grim line. Sighing heavily, he made his decision.

"There was a girl," he began, and felt her slight jerk beside him. He turned to her, noting her look of surprise. "She reminded me a lot of you. Sweet like you." His voice dropped lower. "Innocent like you." His jaw pulsed as he thought about that time. "But then she had that virtue stripped away. By a man she trusted." He heard her hissed intake of breath.

"Oh, Adam. I'm so sorry. Was she...was she special to you?"

How to answer that question? "Not...not in the way you mean."

She patiently waited for him to continue, and he appreciated her forbearance. It wasn't something that was easy to talk about.

"It was while I was in the Dakota Territories. I had decided to winter in a small town called Indian Wells. The people seemed nice and friendly, and there was a church with a preacher. It had been a long time since I had been able to worship in a true church with other believers."

He hesitated, a flood of anger once again raging through him. Amanda placed her small hand against his larger one and gave a reassuring squeeze. He had to choke down the knot that formed in his throat at the simple gesture. He turned his palm up, clinging to her hand as though it were a lifeline back to reality.

"Her name was Lillie," he said, trying to clear the husk from his voice. "Like you, she was nineteen years old. We became friends—more than friends."

He wondered why her hand suddenly trembled against his.

"One day, she went to the church early to set up for the social they were going to have that evening. She was alone, and the preacher...the preacher..." He stopped, unable to continue. He saw Amanda's horrified look, and he quickly turned away from her liquid violet eyes.

"I wanted to kill him," he spat contemptuously. "I did shoot him, and I spent two years in prison for it."

Quiet reigned for several long heartbeats. "That's why you disappeared for so long."

He nodded, feeling as though he had been wrung out and left to dry. "I didn't want anyone to know, so I didn't write or contact anyone."

"What about me?"

He could hear the hurt in her voice and winced. "Especially you. I didn't want you to know the monster I had become."

"How can you say that?" she argued hotly. "You're not a monster, Adam. You could never be a monster."

He tried to pull away, but she wouldn't let him. She gave him a lightning glance, a certain conviction filling her face. "There's more to the story, isn't there? You're not capable of shooting a man in cold blood."

His mouth tilted wryly. Leave it to Amanda to get to the heart of the matter.

"When Lillie accused the preacher, the whole town turned against her, even her own father. They didn't believe her."

Those rosy red lips thinned into a tight line, but she waited for him to continue.

"The preacher attacked her again one night when she was returning home from work. I found them struggling together in an alley."

He could feel the heat creeping through his body just as it had at the time. His anger that had always been such a thorn in his flesh had been kindled into a wildfire.

"I pulled him off her and flung him aside. While I was trying to see if Lillie was all right, the preacher clubbed me with a board. It stunned me for a second, but when I saw him coming at me again, I shot him."

"Oh, Adam." The sympathy in Amanda's eyes did much to lessen the self-condemnation he had been struggling with for the past three years. "You're not the monster. That preacher is."

Her approbation was a soothing balm to his wounded spirit.

"He didn't die when I shot him, but someone else shot him several days later and he did die then. I was accused, tried and sent to prison for a murder I didn't commit."

"Oh, Adam!" she breathed again. "I'm so sorry." She moved closer, placing her other palm against his back. He could see her struggling with something to say that would lessen the pain. She squeezed his hand and he turned away from her look of pity. He didn't need or want anyone's pity.

"The Good Lord says…"

"Don't!" he interrupted savagely, inwardly wincing at her shocked reaction to his anger. "Just…don't."

She sat back, sighing softly in capitulation.

"What happened to Lillie?" she asked quietly.

He blew out a long breath, watching the dancing flames of the fire. "She...disappeared."

Silence reigned for several long seconds. He could tell she didn't know what to say. He was relieved he had confessed it to her, but it didn't make him feel any better about himself.

Instead of speaking, she placed her hands on each side of his face and imbued that touch with all the sympathy and love he knew she was capable of.

His whole being reacted to her touch. Heaven help him, he was no different from that preacher. Something had changed in the way he now saw Amanda, and whenever he looked at her, all kinds of feelings he shouldn't be having surged through him.

Chapter 9

Amanda stared in surprise at Adam's rigid back as he retreated into the darkness beyond the fire. He had jumped up, nearly tumbling over himself, as though a spark from the fire had reached out and branded him. The self-loathing she saw on his face before he turned away troubled her greatly. Surely he didn't think she condemned him for shooting a man in self-defense? Were she in the same situation, she felt fairly certain she would have done the same. He had nothing to reproach himself for.

She didn't mean to sound preachy, but she had been about to remind him the Bible says that vengeance is the Lord's and that He will repay. It shocked and angered her that a person who represented God and His word here on this earth could do such a thing to an innocent woman. As protective of her as Adam had always been, she could well understand his fury over the incident. But she was even more shocked that a congregation of God's people would let the man get away with it.

A jingling of a harness in the distance let her know that Macy was returning with the supplies to fix the stage. At least they hoped it was fixable, or else they would have to spend more time in this isolated area until something else could be arranged. Unless they all piled into the wagon and returned to Blackburn's station, leaving the broken stage behind.

She joined Adam near the stage as Macy drew up in a wagon. The other man climbed down from the vehicle and handed supplies to Adam, who took and dropped them beside the broken axle.

Macy handed Amanda the lantern, and they both joined Adam.

Macy studied the broken coach and lifted an eyebrow at Adam. "Well, let's get to work." He turned to Amanda. "Since this is going to cost in time, I brought vittles for the folk. They'll have to eat now instead of at Blackburn's station."

The others were in varying degrees of wakefulness beside the fire, having heard the approaching vehicle.

The cold seeped into Amanda's bones. She longed to return to her spot by the fire, but she had to keep watch over the mail while the men worked on the coach.

As though he could read her mind, Adam looked up at her from his kneeling position where he was already removing the broken wheel hub.

"I've got this. Go and hand out the food. And make sure you eat something yourself."

The command in his voice made her hackles rise with indignation, but one look into those shifting hazel eyes and she read the concern that prompted the order. Pushing down her irritation, she nodded and went to the other wagon to get the food.

Macy followed her, leaping with agility into the back of the wagon. He lifted out a basket loaded with ham-filled biscuits that, in the distance he had just traversed, probably rendered them like hardtack. He also handed her an extra canteen of water to go along with it. She smiled her thanks and headed in the direction of the fire while he returned to help Adam.

She handed out their meal, such as it was, and settled herself closer to the fire, teeth chattering with the freezing temperatures.

Rose was huddled in her blanket so close to the fire Amanda feared that with the least little movement, she would surely set herself ablaze.

Evan was seated next to her, his arm wrapped around her shoulder to share his body heat. His concern for his sister had been obvious all through this trip, and Amanda wondered what it would have been like to have a brother or sister. Her mother had been unable to bear more children, hence her parents' suffocating protectiveness.

Still, Adam had always been there to fill the void. She couldn't have asked for a better brother, or a better friend. Her lips curled. He could be irritatingly bossy when he wanted to be, but she wouldn't have traded him for a dozen sisters.

Time ticked slowly by and the sun was peeking up over the eastern horizon when Adam and Macy finally finished repairing the coach.

When everyone was loaded back into the stagecoach, Amanda took her place next to Adam on the driver's seat. For this leg of the journey, Adam would be the driver, and she would conduct.

Hollis climbed onto the wagon with Macy, still glaring darkly at Amanda. She lifted her chin and gave him back glare for glare until the man finally looked away.

Adam snapped the reins, starting out at a much slower pace. He refused to take any more chances with the rugged road even though they were now traveling in broad daylight.

Using the pocket watch Mr. Dailey had given her, Amanda noted their time of departure in the logbook.

She could sense Adam's tension and wondered at its cause.

"You'll do fine," she assured him, squeezing his hand reassuringly. "Even though you've never driven this part of the route before, it's very clearly marked."

He glanced at their clasped hands, his mouth thinning with obvious annoyance. Using the excuse of adjusting the reins, he moved his hand out from under hers, leaving her unaccountably hurt by his physical rejection.

"It's not a problem," he agreed, yet still the tension remained.

Before long, they passed from the forest into the prairie, which spread out before them in undulating waves of brown and gold.

Amanda was thankful for the sun beating down on her back; it lessened the freezing chill of the icy air as they flew along. Frosty ringlets puffed out from the surging mules as their huffing breath filled the morning silence.

Macy and Hollis weren't far behind. Amanda could just see them in the distance.

"Do you want to tell me what happened with Hollis?" Adam asked.

The thought of the man's disrespectful attitude angered her all over again.

"I suggested that he slow down and, instead, he spurred the mules to greater speed."

"I thought it might be something like that." He glanced at her and grinned. "Got your feathers in a ruffle, did he?"

She snorted. "He did more than get my feathers in a ruffle, as you put it."

He laughed outright at that. "I thought for a minute there you were going to take the bullwhip to him."

"The thought had crossed my mind," she agreed darkly,

and his laughter rang out again. It was so good to hear his laughter, even more vibrant with his baritone voice than when he was a young man. Whatever had been bothering him earlier seemed to have disappeared, at least for the time being.

Despite the frigid temperatures, Amanda enjoyed this time alone with Adam. He was totally relaxed behind the reins, spurring the mules to greater speed when they reached the open prairie.

As the sun rose higher, the temperatures warmed until Amanda was able to put away the blanket she had been huddling under. She wondered how Adam could seem so impervious to the biting cold, but assumed it had something to do with being male.

It was as though that thought had opened the door to her mind, allowing other thoughts to escape—thoughts she had been holding firmly in check.

It had been years since she had seen Adam. When he had walked into Mr. Dailey's office, she had barely recognized him. The tall, gangly youth who had left when he was just seventeen years old had metamorphosed into an even taller and more muscular man.

Every inch of him exuded pure, male dominance. Unlike before when they were children, when he grew angry with her now, she was truly intimidated. Those warm hazel eyes had hardened into something she couldn't quite put a name to.

After hearing his story, she could well understand why, but she missed the camaraderie they had shared growing up. At first, he had seemed glad to see her. Now she wasn't so certain.

They pulled into Blackburn's station, and Adam jumped down to check on his repair job while Mr. Blackburn quickly exchanged mules. He joined Adam, looking over his shoulder at the wheel.

"Will it hold?"

Adam sighed. He stood and faced the other man. "It will have to. Macy told me you didn't have another coach here."

Mr. Blackburn shook his head. "Nope. You won't find another one until Colbert's Ferry, although it's possible you might find one at Waddell. I heard Butterfield was sending out extra coaches for spots along the way."

Another man joined them and Blackburn turned to introduce them.

"This here's Dan Sutton. He'll be your new driver."

Adam's inspection of the man was returned in full, and they exchanged an accepting nod. They both seemed to like what they were seeing. Something about the old coot appealed to Adam, though he couldn't for the life of him say why.

Amanda climbed down from the coach, ready to be introduced, as well. Adam made the introductions, and Amanda smiled warmly at the old man.

Old he might be, but his posture radiated confidence, and his stocky body had weathered the years well.

Amanda turned to Mr. Blackburn. Adam recognized the look on her face. It was the same look she wore whenever she thought she was going to have to do battle to get her way.

"Mr. Hollis has been fired," she told Blackburn with no hesitancy in her voice.

Blackburn merely nodded. "I'll let the superintendent know and get a replacement."

"You don't seem surprised," Adam told him.

"Naw. Been expecting it. Everett Hollis ain't got the sense God gave a cricket."

Adam decided not to ask why. They were already behind schedule.

"Let's go," he urged the others. "Time's a wastin'."

When Amanda would have climbed up beside the driver, he held her back. "My turn. Remember?"

She looked so woebegone he had to grin. It was definitely more pleasant riding on the outside than on the inside of the coach. He saw the pleading in her eyes and didn't have the heart to refuse that unspoken request.

"All right. Climb up."

Her smile warmed him more effectively than the intensifying sun. He helped her up and took his place beside her, nodding to Sutton they were ready to begin.

It was a tight fit with the three of them squished together on one small seat, but Amanda took up very little room. Still, Adam placed an arm behind her back to give her a bit more space. When she snuggled into his side, the warmth from her body and the soft fragrance of her hair tangled with his senses, making his breath catch in his throat. It suddenly occurred to him this was not such a good idea, but since Sutton had already set the coach in motion, it was too late to do anything about it now.

Sutton wrinkled his nose at the azure-blue sky. "Ah, the Good Lord sure set a fine day for travelin'."

Adam closed his eyes and huffed out a breath. *Great. Another one.*

Amanda leaned back and grinned up into his face, and he had no trouble reading what was in her mind. He frowned in warning but, as usual, she chose to ignore him.

"I agree, Mr. Sutton. A mighty fine day," she chirruped.

The old man gave her a swift glance. "Call me Dan."

Amanda's smile lit her face, and Adam sighed inwardly. It was going to be a long one hundred and twenty miles.

"All right, Dan. And you may call me A…Manny."

Sutton frowned. "Amanny? That's an unusual name."

Adam smiled down at her blushing face.

"No. It's just Manny."

Sutton nodded slowly, a confused look still on his face. "Right."

Amanda changed the subject by pointing to some animals off to their right. Adam and Sutton followed her pointing finger.

"Antelope," Sutton told her.

"They're beautiful!"

"Good eating, too."

Adam pressed his lips together to keep from laughing outright at Amanda's appalled expression. She glared a don't-you-dare-laugh-at-me look his way, which only made it harder not to.

"'These are the beasts which ye shall eat; the ox, the sheep, and the goat, the hart, and the roebuck, and the fallow deer, and the wild goat, and the pygarg, and the wild ox, and the chamois.'" Sutton spit a wad of tobacco juice with unerring accuracy at a scorpion as they flashed by it. "Had a missionary tell me that that there pygarg was the same as an antelope."

He fastened his sprightly blue eyes on Amanda, expecting some kind of comment on his sagacity. She didn't disappoint him.

"How interesting," she said lamely.

From then on, he kept up a running commentary on scriptures and *the Good Lord* that lasted through the next two stops, which constituted the better part of four hours. Though irritated, Adam was impressed. As uneducated as the man was, he could quote scriptures better than most preachers he knew.

They made it to Colbert's Ferry without incident. Adam saw to the changing of the coaches while Amanda made certain to see the mail was transferred.

The passengers disembarked for the meal being provided at this location.

The Colbert station was owned and operated by George

Colbert, who was half Scot and half Chickasaw. He was a young man, not yet thirty, yet he was already on his third wife.

His farm boasted a fine yield of corn, which was being cared for by several African slaves. Others in the distance were cutting away the sand of the Red River near the banks to give easier access to the waterway. Several men worked on the beginnings of what would one day be a bridge, but as for now, they would cross by ferry, which was merely a log raft pushed across by men with long poles. Nothing they hadn't seen before.

Adam sent Amanda inside to eat while he finished seeing to the hitching of the teams. He covertly watched her walk away, inhaling the first real breath he had taken for the past several miles. His growing attraction to Amanda was seriously beginning to concern him.

Amanda, unaware of these thoughts, hurried inside the station house, hoping to be able to finish eating quickly so that Adam could take his turn.

The passengers were all arranged around a long table, the smell of the food reaching Amanda seconds before she arrived at her seat. Her stomach growled its appreciation.

It was obvious that Colbert didn't skimp on supplies. There was even butter for the biscuits and sugar for the coffee.

Mrs. Colbert handed Amanda a plate as soon as she seated herself. Amanda smiled her appreciation and quickly dug in.

The marshal was already scarfing down a piece of peach pie and, for the first time in a long while, no one was complaining, too intent on making the best of what would in all probability be the last good meal they received until San Francisco.

When Sutton entered the house, Amanda quickly rose

to her feet and headed outside. She found Adam leaning against the new stage, staring at the workers in the distance.

"Your turn," she told him, but he didn't move. "Adam, you have to eat," she admonished softly.

He turned on her a look full of frustration, and she blinked rapidly, trying to figure out the cause.

"Is something wrong?"

He stared at her for several long seconds, as though he was trying to make up his mind whether to make her privy to his thoughts, before he finally shook his head.

"No. Nothing."

He pushed past her and headed into the station, and she frowned at his retreating back, wondering what in the world she had done now to put that look on his face.

Shaking her head, she turned back to watch the slaves as they loaded the coach onto the ferry. As she stared, the coach arriving from Sherman, Texas, pulled up on the Texas bank of the river, which sent everyone on this side scurrying to get the ferry under way.

Amanda squinted at the sun, which was now a bright globe high in the sky. Even though they had traveled much of the time in the darkness, they had never had an accident until Hollis decided he wanted to show off his driving skills. Traveling at night was an eerie experience, especially when the darkened landscape was invisible to the naked eye. She much preferred traveling in the day.

They managed to cross the Red River without incident and were quickly on their way to Sherman, Texas.

She didn't know why Adam had suddenly become so quiet, but whatever was bothering him, she wished he would just come out and say it. The tension was making her as wound up as a tightly coiled spring.

Chapter 10

The farther west they traveled, the more Adam could sense an increasing tension in Sutton. The man's searching gaze became more intense, his jovial voice dropping more often into silence.

"Something bothering you?" he finally asked.

The old man spit tobacco juice off to the side, his eyes quickly scanning in every direction. "We're coming into Comanche territory."

Amanda jerked against Adam's side, and he dropped his arm from the seat back to rest it around her shoulders, giving her a reassuring squeeze, although he hardly felt reassured himself.

"Is there a problem?" she asked, the trepidation in her voice coming through crystal clear despite her attempts to seem unconcerned.

It was hard for Adam to stay focused on the conversation when every fiber of his being was blazingly aware of the soft contours of Amanda's body snuggled so close to his own. If he was in danger, he had a feeling it had more to do with his tangled feelings for the woman at his side than any outside source.

Sutton sighed, answering Amanda's question rather reluctantly. "You might say that. A Comanche war party attacked the coach last week."

Amanda sucked in a sharp breath. "Was anybody hurt?"

Sutton exchanged a quick look with Adam, and his stomach plunged at the look in the other man's eyes. Voice devoid of emotion, Sutton pursed his lips and told her, "Everybody was killed and the coach was stolen."

Adam felt the shock of that statement all the way down to his toes. He joined Sutton in searching out the landscape.

Setting Amanda away from him, he picked up his rifle and quickly checked it over. He pulled his ammunition bag closer, placing it between his legs.

Amanda watched him a minute then hurriedly pulled out her pistol and did the same.

Sutton nodded at them. "Good idea. Never hurts to be prepared."

Adam gave himself a mental kick. He should never have agreed to this trip. Why hadn't he done a little more investigating before assenting to this cockamamy scheme of traipsing off into the unknown? He felt helpless knowing he had no control over whatever they might encounter. It was at times like this he wanted to call on God for help, but he didn't think it was right to talk to Him only when he needed something. His bitterness had severed that connection long ago.

He glanced at Amanda, knowing if they were attacked by a large party of Indians, they were hopelessly outnumbered. The responsibility for the others in the stage suddenly rested heavily upon his shoulders. If he had to die defending them, then so be it. He prayed only that when the time came, he was capable enough.

The desire to pour out his heart to God became suddenly overwhelming. His past had taught him the Lord didn't really care enough to intercede on his behalf, yet, despite what he had said earlier, he couldn't bring himself to fully deny that Power.

He would try anything to keep Amanda from coming to harm.

Lord, it's my fault for not listening in the first place to that still, small voice You put in my head. I should have known better. Whatever happens, if You won't listen to me, please remember how much Amanda loves You and keep her safe.

Remembering Lillie, he blew out a bitter sigh.

Amanda watched the fierce look that came to Adam's eyes. Why, oh why, had she wanted to do such a crazy thing as conducting a stage across miles and miles of treacherous, practically uncharted territory? With each passing mile, her reasons for doing so became murkier, much like the Red River they had recently crossed.

They soon reached the small but growing town of Sherman, and the superintendent himself was there with a new team of mules. It took only moments, and they were on their way again.

Of all the drivers they had had thus far, Dan Sutton was Amanda's favorite. The old man had one of the cheeriest dispositions of anyone she had ever known.

Like her, he had noticed that something seemed to be bothering Adam.

"Somethin' on your mind, son?"

Adam glanced at him, at Amanda and quickly away.

"Nothing worth talking about."

Sutton studied Adam with a lifted brow, but instead of continuing the conversation, he nodded. "All right."

The silence became almost oppressive. At the next stop, Sutton would be leaving them and a new driver would be taking over. Amanda wished it could be otherwise, but she understood the reasoning behind Butterfield's policy of changing drivers. She had been thoroughly impressed with how well they knew their routes. They could practically tell you if a rock had moved, so in tune were they with their section of landscape.

But Sutton was different. Behind that rough face, scrawny beard and twinkling eyes, this was a man familiar with, and comfortable with, God. He not only saw the landscape, but also the One who created it. He continually pointed out various items of interest she would have otherwise overlooked, and he always gave credit to *the Good Lord*. If Adam thought she used the pithy saying too much, he must be just about ready to pull his hair out after the past fifty miles.

The rolling prairie spread out before them, covered in a fine layer of grass; intermittent shrubs dotted the landscape for as far as the eye could see. A jackrabbit scuttled away at their approach, and a hawk screamed in the sky as it recognized a familiar prey.

Temperatures continued to rise as the day progressed. Amanda shucked her leather jacket, lifting her face to the warm breeze that crossed their path.

In the distance, dust rose in the air in a little, puffy cloud. Sutton's spiky brows drew down to meet between his eyes.

"What do you think it is?" Amanda asked him, the man's alert posture making goose bumps tingle across her arms in warning.

Adam, too, was watching the growing cloud of dust as it moved ever closer.

Their increased tension had her unhooking the safety strap that held her pistol in its holster.

"Is it a dust storm?" she asked, one hand shading her eyes against the bright sun. A cold sense of foreboding shivered through her as images of men on horseback began to take shape among the rolling sand.

Adam suddenly grabbed for his rifle at the same time Sutton picked up his bullwhip and snapped it with urgency over the backs of the already straining mules.

"Hyah! Git up there."

Amanda was thrown off balance, slamming into Adam's side. Grabbing the footrest of the wagon, she pulled herself off him, struggling to gain her balance as the mules fought against the whip. Inside, shouted protests could be heard as the coach picked up speed and rocked and swayed over the bumpy ground.

Sutton turned the mules aside, and the dust cloud turned also on an intercept course.

Amanda finally understood just what she was seeing, and a cold chill raced up and down her spine. It was entirely possible the Indians approaching were friendly, but it was just as likely they were not. The way the horses were bearing down on them didn't exactly inspire confidence.

"Are they Comanche?" she asked Dan, barely above a whisper.

"Don't know, and don't intend to wait around and find out."

The whip cracked again, but the tiring mules with the loaded-down wagon were no match for the rapidly approaching Indians.

"My revolver will be no use until they are close, and by then it may be too late," she told Adam, reminding him that his was the only rifle.

Sutton drew a ten-gauge coach gun from under the seat and tossed it to her. "Ever use one of these?" he asked.

Amanda hadn't, but she guessed she was about to learn. She had always heard that the recoil from the sawed-off shotgun was enough to send a full-grown man flying backward; she could only wonder what it would do to her.

"Give it here," Adam yelled, handing her his rifle. At any other time, she might have argued, wanting to show her ability and independence, but this was neither the time nor the place. Frankly, this trip was teaching her a lot more about herself and her own inadequacies than the reverse.

This was going to be a tricky situation. Butterfield agents were forbidden to fire on Indians unless their lives were in danger, and by the time they figured that out, it just might be too late. The ones approaching didn't look as if they were a small party.

"Sit," Adam snapped, jerking her down beside him. She hadn't realized she had risen to her feet to get a better view of the oncoming riders.

Their war cries reached them seconds before an arrow seemed to sprout from the seat right between Amanda's legs. Her shocked look met Adam's equally stunned one, and she wondered if her face was as white as his. Regret flashed in those hazel orbs before he quickly turned his attention to the approaching horses.

She tried to balance herself and take aim, but it was going to be a lot harder to hit a moving target when she was moving herself. She focused on the lead rider, his half-clad figure expertly holding on with his legs while nocking an arrow onto his bow.

Gunfire coming from inside the coach told her the marshal must have entered the fray.

Amanda sighted on the brave, her finger curling slowly around the trigger. She was frozen in indecision. There was a big difference between shooting at targets and shooting a human being. She had never taken a life before, not even for the stew pot.

"Shoot!" Adam yelled.

Her hesitation allowed the Indian to get off his shot, and it flew with precision, imbedding itself into Sutton's chest. A gurgle emitted from his throat as he clutched the arrow, struggling to keep from keeling over and releasing his control on the reins.

Horrified, Amanda reflexively gripped Sutton's shoulder to keep him from pitching out of the flying stage. At the same time, she tried to wrest the reins from his fierce grip, struggling not to lose her own hold on the rifle.

Adam snatched the rifle from Amanda, freeing her to look after Sutton. He quickly took aim and, with no hesitation whatsoever, began firing. The lead rider went down with Adam's first shot, but the others kept coming. Amanda counted nine more fully painted men.

"Get us out of here!" Adam yelled. He quickly reloaded his rifle, bringing down a second rider with his next shot.

Another arrow sliced through the overhead canvas of the coach, and Rose screamed. Amanda prayed no one had been hit. More and more, she was feeling the responsibility of her rash actions.

She pulled Sutton to a position between herself and Adam, wedging him in as much as possible. Blood oozed from where the arrow protruded from his chest, too close to his heart for comfort. Every instinct within her wanted to remove that arrow and patch the wound, but that was an impossibility when all of their lives depended on getting out of the area as fast as possible.

The warriors were closer now, so close Amanda could see the glittering hate in their dark eyes. As they moved alongside the coach, Adam pulled her gun from the holster where it rested on her hip and fired off five rapid shots with unerring accuracy.

Three braves fell from their horses, two others pulling back as they struggled to stay seated on their animals after having been shot.

What was left of the entire raiding party stopped, staring after the fast-receding coach, their war cries now silenced as they were left behind in a cloud of dust. The astonished looks on the faces of the remaining Indians would have been funny if not for the seriousness of the situation. Amanda was more thankful than ever she had taken the prototype pistol from her father's safe. Its repeating action had surely saved their lives.

Amanda kept control of the mules as Adam inspected the depth of injury to Sutton. The old man had passed out long ago, and the only thing that had kept him from sliding off the seat was his position between her and Adam.

When she judged it safe enough, Amanda pulled back on the reins, sending up a little prayer the mules would respond. The wagon eased to a stop. At any other time, she would have had to struggle with the normally stubborn beasts, but now the mules stood with heaving sides, their heads hanging low to the ground.

Mr. Bass hesitantly opened the door and peered around. His white face stood out against the golden background of the prairie as he quickly scanned the surrounding area.

"Are we safe?" he asked.

"Bass," Adam yelled. "Give me a hand here."

The other man scrambled from the coach and came to the front of the wagon. Amanda climbed down and, with Mr. Bass's assistance, helped Adam lower Sutton to the ground.

The marshal had climbed out after Mr. Bass, his prisoner still handcuffed to his side.

Amanda looked up. "Where are the Nightingtons?" she asked anxiously.

The marshal shrugged. "The woman is currently having a fit of hysterics and her brother is trying to calm her."

Her whole body shaking, Amanda would have gladly joined the other woman, but that definitely didn't go along with the image she had been trying to project. After all, it's what she wanted, wasn't it? To be seen as self-reliant?

Able to take care of herself? Or was she simply deluding herself? She wanted nothing more right now than to throw herself into Adam's arms and howl like a coyote.

She was beginning to realize that being a pampered, genteel woman wasn't something entirely undesirable. Here she stood shaking like the leaves in autumn and no one gave her a second glance. Her gaze fell on Sutton's bleeding form, and she felt ashamed for her moment of self-pity.

The arrow had pierced Dan's chest near his collarbone and was protruding from his back.

"Manny, get me some of the clean rags from the medical bag."

Amanda hurried to retrieve the small bag of medical supplies that the stages carried. She handed it to Adam and then knelt beside him.

"What can I do to help?"

Adam surreptitiously studied Amanda to see if she was all right. Now was not the time to jerk her into his arms and hold her so tightly he'd never let her go, although he wanted to with every fiber of his being. She was trying to give the impression the whole incident hadn't affected her, but her hands were shaking so badly she almost dropped the medical case.

As he worked over the old man, he gave thought to a future he had almost lost. He had seen his life flash before his eyes today, and he didn't like what he had seen. He forced his mind to focus on the problem at hand.

"I'm going to have to break the arrow and pull it out," he told Amanda, hoping she could hold out a little longer. It was clear to him she was on the verge of shock. He gripped her cold fingers, trying to imbue her with some of his own strength. "When I do, put pressure on both sides."

Her face was whiter than he had ever seen it, but she

gave an almost imperceptible nod. Manny was brave to a fault, but today's experiences would have shaken anyone, especially a woman raised in relative isolation to be a lady. Adventurous stories were one thing, firsthand experience quite another.

It was fortunate that Sutton was unconscious. He glanced at Amanda. "Ready?"

She nodded more firmly this time and took a deep breath.

She flinched when he snapped the arrow in two, and again when he slid the two pieces out of Sutton's body. She quickly pressed wadded gauze against the two wounds and held it until he was able to bind them tightly by wrapping strips around Sutton's chest and shoulder. The wounds really needed to be cauterized, but he didn't want to stay in this vicinity any longer than necessary. They weren't out of danger yet.

When they finally had Sutton patched to Adam's satisfaction, Amanda slowly sank back onto the sand, pulling her legs up to her chest. The tortured look in her eyes nearly stopped his heart.

"It's my fault," she whispered. "If Dan dies, it will be all my fault."

He knew why she was thinking that way. "It's not."

She sucked in a hiccupping breath, and he figured she was nearing the threshold of tears. He wanted to hold her so badly, he could feel her phantom warmth in his arms.

"If I hadn't hesitated to shoot, he wouldn't have been shot!"

The tears came now, in an unceasing river of sorrow. She brushed angrily at the moisture sliding down her cheeks.

Oh, how he wanted to comfort her, but he was afraid if he did, she would lose control of the composure she was maintaining by the merest thread. Instead, he rose to his feet and frowned down at her.

"This is neither the time nor the place, Manny. We have to go. Help me get Sutton into the stage."

Her wounded look was like a dagger to the heart. She promptly got to her feet, quickly drying the tears on her face with still-shaking hands and giving him a glare that told him that, for the time being at least, she had mustered a semblance of her old nerve.

He paused at the door of the coach, glancing at Rose Nightington still huddled in her brother's arms, sniffling and gulping. Even with a pink nose and red eyes, the woman was breathtakingly beautiful.

For the first time in their acquaintance, Jake seemed to have lost some of his swagger. He settled down next to the marshal, his eyes darting about in an uneasy examination of everyone in the coach. The thought that he very nearly could have lost his scalp must have affected him more than Adam thought possible.

Even Mr. Bass was unusually tense. Although nothing seemed to affect the man's formidable composure, his color was still alarmingly white.

"You okay?" Adam asked.

He met Adam's eyes briefly and nodded. "I'm fine."

They quickly folded down the middle seat and, as gently as possible, laid Sutton inside the coach, which forced Mr. Bass to sit crunched on one side with the Nightingtons, and the mail parcels that had been seatmates with Mr. Bass to be piled against the marshal and Jake.

Amanda took the reins, staring straight ahead, her lips pressed tightly together. Adam sighed soundlessly. He would have to make things right with her, but now was not the time. Hopefully, when they reached the next station, she would have realized he hadn't meant to hurt her.

Chapter 11

The next station was rather primitive in its amenities, but they were able to cauterize Sutton's wound and patch it. He was carefully placed on the bed in the backroom of the depot the mail agents used for sleeping. This was the old man's last stop before a new driver took over, so the trip would go on unimpeded, leaving him behind to hopefully recover. He was a fighter, but his age was telling on him.

Amanda pulled the quilt over him and then sat on the rough bed, taking his cold, gnarled hand into her own.

"I am so sorry," she told him.

He returned the pressure on her hand, his serious, faded eyes focusing on hers. "It's not your fault, Manny," he disagreed, his voice a mere thread. "It ain't easy to take a life, especially not the first time."

That thought did little to assuage her guilt. Having seen Adam in action, it made her pause for thought. Adam had shot those Indians with a quick instinct that made her wonder just exactly what he had been doing with the past few years of his life when he hadn't been in jail. There had been no hesitation whatsoever on his part. It had reminded her of the stories she had heard of lawless gunslingers. But that was not Adam. That *couldn't* be Adam.

"So where was your Good Lord today, old man?"

Amanda nearly jumped out of her skin. She hadn't heard Adam enter the little room. The anger in his voice surprised her. She tried to catch his eye in warning, but he refused to look at her.

"He was there, son," Sutton answered softly.

Adam's lips pressed together. "Yeah. He took real good care of you, didn't He?"

"Adam!"

Amanda was appalled at his callousness.

"It's all right," Sutton said, patting Amanda's hand. When he fixed his glaring eyes on Adam, there was nothing of an invalid in that look. "It ain't the Good Lord's fault that I chose to drive a stage in Indian Territory. I know the risks, and I choose to take them. The Good Lord gave me a brain and it's up to me whether I use it or not." His glance bounced between Adam and Amanda. "Did you know the risks when you came on board?"

Amanda could almost see Adam's anger deflate at the question.

Sutton's glare became fiercer. "So you think humanity should be allowed to do as they please and that God, the most awesome creator of the universe, the holiest of holies, should just follow us around and clean up our messes like some good little slave?"

Amanda cringed at the thought. Glancing at Adam, she could see that, like her, he had never really considered such an idea. She was the one being deceitful toward her parents. She was the one who had begged to be included in this journey. Something within her had tried to hold her back, but she had ignored that warning and blithely chose to go her own way. If something happened to her on this trip, it surely wasn't God's fault.

Neither she nor Adam could give Sutton an answer.

When Adam's hazel eyes finally connected with hers, she frowned at their glittering hardness. "We need to leave," he said roughly.

It took every ounce of courage she could muster to release Sutton's hand and get up off the bed. Days and days of endless travel in a coach that rode like a bucking bronco, never getting enough sleep, never being really clean, never getting enough to eat, was wearing on her more than she had anticipated. On top of that, the Comanche had been worrisome enough, but now they were headed into Apache territory.

As though sensing her hesitation, Sutton patted her hand again before releasing it. "Don't you worry none. The Good Lord is with you no matter what happens. He doesn't promise we won't have to pay for our own mistakes, only that He will be with us no matter the outcome."

Despite everything, those words brought her comfort.

When Adam looked at the old man, the tense planes of his face relaxed and the hardness in his eyes softened, reminding her more of the man she used to know. He gripped Sutton's hand with both of his, shaking them together. "You get well, you old coot."

"You take care of this little lady, you hear me? Or you'll have me to answer to!"

Adam's lips tilted into a one-sided smile. He turned and quickly left the room. Amanda bent and kissed the old man's cheek. Without saying anything else, she walked out the door, tears clogging her throat. She hated to leave Sutton behind. She would miss his godly tirades.

While Adam checked the harnesses, she made notes in the journal, sniffing back tears trying to force their way out. When she finished writing, she stared blankly at the surrounding terrain. She shivered in the steadily decreasing temperatures as the sun once again began its descent, the bleak and barren landscape only adding to the cold feeling.

Adam joined her a moment later, his expression questioning. "Are you all right?"

Without looking at him, she took a deep breath and slowly released it, the cold air causing her hot breath to turn into a cloud of vapor around her face. Shaking her head, she said, "I can't do it, Adam."

He didn't say anything, but she felt him move, and then she was turned around and wrapped tightly in his arms. He nestled her head under his chin and simply held her.

She tried counting to ten to hold back the emotion, but before she reached five, the tears were sliding down her cheeks in a silent river of sorrow. She wanted nothing more right now than to stand here like this for the rest of her life. If only it were that simple.

"A lot has happened in the past days, and you're tired. We all are. You're stronger than you realize. You *can* do this!"

She sucked in a breath, her bottom lip quivering. "I'm not strong like you. I thought I was, but I'm not."

"Oh, Manny, Manny." He sighed. "Why are you always trying to be something you're not?"

She stiffened in his arms, but when she tried to pull away, he wouldn't allow it.

"No. Listen to me. You are a woman, one of the most gentle and loving I have ever known. God made women to be nurturers, just as He made men to be the protectors and providers. There's nothing wrong with being feminine, Manny, and that's what you are, no matter how you dress, no matter how well you shoot a gun."

She tilted her head back so she could see his rugged face. "Is that truly how you see me? As some weak little female?"

He snorted, his hazel eyes crinkling with laughter. "Manny, there's not a weak bone in your body. Being feminine doesn't make you weak," he chided. "Women have strengths that men can only guess at, and vice versa. We are who God created us to be."

She saw surprise cross his features when he realized what he had said. He studied her face as though memorizing every detail. His eyes grew darker, and she wondered what strong emotion had him in its grip. Something flashed through his eyes. She couldn't catch it quickly enough to decide what it was, but her heart thrummed violently in response.

"I say, can you give me a hand?"

At the sound of Evan's voice, Adam released her as though he had been scalded. She watched as he struggled with whatever sentiments had stung him, fighting his thoughts until the pupils of his eyes retracted and their hazel color once again emerged. Amanda had to envy him such control; she was still a vibrating mass of conflicted emotions. Adam turned to Evan.

"What?"

The other man's eyes widened at the brusqueness of the query. He eyed Adam warily.

"My sister is in hysterics. She refuses to budge from this location. She wants to go back. Will you talk to her? She'll listen to you."

Adam glanced briefly at Amanda before following Evan to where they could hear Rose sobbing near the stage, refusing to climb inside.

Amanda followed more slowly, her legs still shaking from that brief moment she was held in Adam's arms. For an instant, she thought Adam had been about to kiss her. Even the thought of it made her mouth go dry and her heart accelerate until she could see tiny black dots dancing before her eyes. She needed to slow her breathing or she was surely about to swoon.

When she rounded the stage, she stopped dead in her tracks. Adam stood with his arms wrapped around Rose very much as he had held Amanda seconds before. The other woman clung to Adam like a whimpering leech. Amanda was surprised with a primitive urge to tear Rose from Adam's hold.

He was murmuring to her, his voice so low Amanda couldn't make out the words. Whatever he was saying was having an effect because the hysterical wailing stopped, only to be replaced with a whimpering acceptance.

Adam finally got Rose settled down enough that he was able to wrangle her into the coach. When he started to move backward, her eyes flew to his and he recognized the returning panic. She latched on to his hand and refused to let go.

"Please! Don't go. Ride inside with us."

Rose's obvious attempts to attract his attention hadn't gone unnoticed by him. He couldn't call himself any kind of man if he wasn't flattered by her interest, but if this was another ploy to do so, he didn't have the time. He noticed a bank of clouds to the west and could smell a change in the air. He was afraid they were headed for some bad weather.

He met Amanda's fierce look, and his eyes widened in surprise. Her violet eyes fairly glistened with some kind of primeval emotion. If he didn't know better, he would think Amanda was jealous. And why did that thought give him so much pleasure?

When Evan joined Amanda, taking her attention away from him, Adam was fairly certain the same emotion now rushed through his own body.

A few moments ago, when he had held her, her vulnerability had opened a chasm in his heart that had been sealed shut for years. The emotional lava of his hidden feelings had spilled forth, flowing through him in an ever-increasing tide until he thought those same feelings were about to engulf him.

The look in Amanda's eyes told him his feelings were reciprocated, but she was too naive to realize what was happening. Thank Amanda's Good Lord that Evan had interrupted or he wasn't certain what might have happened. Until this trip was over, he was her protector and nothing more. He must stay focused on the objective—get to San Francisco—or they could all be in trouble.

To give himself some space from the volatile emotions Amanda incited, he decided to acquiesce to Rose's plea and ride inside the coach.

He seated himself next to Mr. Bass and across from the Nightingtons, squirming uncomfortably under Rose's enamored gaze. They were quickly on their way again, and it didn't take long for Adam to realize he had made a big mistake. Rose took his compliance to her pleading as a sign he was equally interested in her.

He carefully studied her now, realizing that she was, indeed, a very beautiful woman. Her bout with hysterics had done nothing toward diminishing her beauty. If anything, her tears had brightened her eyes to a shimmering blue that he had never seen before, and the pinkness of her nose from weeping only emphasized its delicate structure. And yet, her exquisite beauty left him entirely unmoved. Instead, Amanda's face crowded his thoughts, making him realize something for the first time: his heart and soul were bound to his little rebel. He had been fighting it for years without realizing it.

What Sutton had said about being created as God meant for us to be had helped Adam understand. Wasn't there a scripture that discussed kicking against the goads? That's what he had been doing for years, fighting the very person God had created him to be. That was why he could never settle down. No matter where his body went, his heart had been in Tennessee with a feisty little woman who had stolen that organ years before. His childish desire to protect her had turned into a man's desire to possess her.

He understood better now why no woman had ever been able to keep his interest. Once they became serious about him, he had felt compelled to run. Staring into Rose's luminous eyes, that feeling once again overcame him but, for the time being, there was nowhere to run to.

Amanda sat beside the driver, her emotions in turmoil. Mile after mile she berated herself for her unruly thoughts. How on earth had she gotten to the point where common sense eluded her?

Seeing Rose batting her baby-blue eyes at Adam had given her a wild, childish desire to tear the other woman's hair out by the roots. Such violent thoughts were uncommon for her. She couldn't remember feeling this strongly about anything ever before. It was rather frightening to know that somewhere buried inside her was a jealous monster fighting to get out.

If she had doubted it before, those doubts had been laid to rest. She loved Adam, and *not* like a sister. Her experience with men had been limited, but she knew enough to recognize he felt some kind of attraction in return. How amazing! What kind, or how deep those feelings went, she had no idea, but she decided right here and now she was going to find out.

Had this been the Good Lord's intention from the very beginning? Or was she simply seeing things she only hoped for?

"We're in for it now."

Her thoughts were brought up short by the warning

voice of the driver. She followed the direction of his gaze, and her heart seemed to stop midbeat. Ominous gray clouds hung low on the western horizon, a portent of the approaching storm they were rapidly heading into.

The driver picked up speed, but Amanda knew they had no hope of outrunning the weather to the next station. The stops between stations had grown in distance the farther west they traveled.

After driving several more miles into the intensifying wind, they were close enough to see ahead of them a blanket of white falling from the sky. The wind in front of the storm began to strengthen the closer they got to it. The ground they were traveling over was bare and brown, but just ahead, there was no way to differentiate the land from the sky.

The driver tucked his hat lower, his face set grimly. "We're heading for a whiteout."

She had heard of the snowstorms that dumped large masses of flaky precipitation until, with the fierce wind blowing it in all directions, getting your bearings was nearly impossible.

"What should we do?"

He spurred the mules into a faster pace. "We go as long as we can, and then we'll have to hole up. The next station is more than twenty miles away."

Amanda clung tightly to the seat as they bounded along, the mules' long-legged pace eating up the miles until, much sooner than she had anticipated, they were swallowed by a white cloud of snow. The chill wind that had constantly bombarded them as they flew along now became frigid with particles of snow, which stung their exposed skin. She huddled into her sheepskin-lined jacket, thankful now she had listened to Adam when he had insisted she buy one in Memphis.

The mules began to balk. Tucking their heads low to

the ground, they bucked in the traces, refusing to move any farther despite the whip the driver wielded with expert ease.

"Get inside the coach," the driver yelled over the screeching wind. "Whatever you do, don't let go of the coach!"

"What about you?" she yelled back, trying to shield her eyes from the blowing ice.

"I'll be in as soon as I see to the mules." He grinned, his teeth showing whitely against his dark beard coated with ice crystals. "Save me a seat."

Amanda backed over the side of the stage, making certain she kept a firm grip on the handles. Before she could reach the ground, large hands encircled her waist and lifted her off the coach.

Her feet touched the ground, and Adam threw his arm around her shoulder, pushing her along until they reached the door of the stage.

Evan reached from inside and grabbed her hands to help her into the carriage while Adam lifted her from behind.

When she no longer felt the warm pressure of Adam's reassuring grip, she panicked. People had been known to die only feet from safety in storms such as these.

"Adam!" she screamed, trying to pull her hands free from Evan.

"Go on!" he yelled from behind. "I need to make certain Sam is all right."

Relieved to hear Adam's reassuring voice, she stopped fighting Evan and tumbled onto the middle seat as he pulled her the rest of the way inside. He quickly closed the canvas behind her, tying the straps to keep the wind from penetrating any farther.

Before long, Adam and Sam climbed into the stage, shivering from the biting cold. Adam seated himself next to Amanda, and Sam wedged himself onto the seat next to Evan. The canvas-topped coach was not meant for weather like this and did very little to keep out the bone-chilling cold.

Except for the fury of the wind, the only sound inside the coach was the heavy breathing of the frightened passengers. The eerie silence was broken by the marshal's voice coming from behind. "So, what's the prognosis?"

Sam spoke up. "We're going to be mighty cozy in here for a while. I recommend you get real friendly with your seatmates and cozy up to each other because our body heat is the only thing between us and freezing to death."

Amanda suddenly wished, for more reasons than one, that she had Rose's layers of clothing. With Adam on one side and Mr. Bass on the other, she was at least better situated than the marshal and Jake.

"Rose, you should move to the middle," Evan told his sister. "You'll be warmer."

Sam grinned at Rose. "That's for certain. I'll make sure you stay toasty warm."

Evan threw him a warning glare that only made Sam grin wider.

Rose speared Amanda, huddled next to Adam, with an envious glance. Without looking at Sam, she reluctantly exchanged seats with her brother.

"You and Jake better climb over and sit on the floor between us," Adam told Marshal Tucker. Seeing the wisdom in such an arrangement, Tucker nodded and, with Jake in tow, awkwardly climbed over the back of the seat between Amanda and Mr. Bass. They settled on the floor among everyone's feet, crowding as close as possible.

Adam wrapped his arm around Amanda and tugged her close to his side. He nodded at Mr. Bass. "Better get close, Bass. Now is no time for propriety, not if we want to be alive when this storm is over."

Bass glanced apologetically at Amanda before shuffling closer on the seat. Using the quilts that had been provided, everyone huddled into little cocoons and settled down to wait out the storm.

Chapter 12

Amanda shivered despite the warm bodies pressed against her, her chattering teeth adding to the symphony of clacking mandibles around her. If they ever got out of this, she was going back to Tennessee and never leaving again! Who would have thought this ever-expanding country could house so many different climates and weather phenomena? She wondered if she would ever be warm again.

"Are you all right?"

Adam's whispered voice against her ear sent a whole different set of shivers waving across her body. She nodded, her clenched teeth unable to release the words she wanted to say.

As long as you are with me, I will always be all right.

She wondered what the end of this trip would mean for her relationship with Adam. Would they revert to the same brother/sister relationship they had before? Perhaps for him, but she didn't think she could ever turn off the feelings her recent awakening had inspired. She was only now beginning to realize the intense longing that had lain dormant in her for so many years.

"Seems to me this trip has been cursed from the beginning," Marshal Tucker stated, his frustrated voice coming from the folds of the quilt he had wrapped about himself.

Amanda couldn't argue with that. Just about everything that could happen to delay them had happened.

"Aw, this ain't s-s-so bad," Sam disagreed, despite his chattering teeth. "I seen w-worse."

Sitting next to the doors, he and Evan were taking the brunt of the cold, along with Mr. Bass and Adam. At least with her body snuggled next to Adam's and Mr. Bass next to her, she was slightly warmer. The same could be true of Rose, as well, if she could come down off her high horse long enough to allow the men beside her to share their body heat. But she pulled as far away from Sam as she could possibly get in the cramped confines of the coach.

Now, if it were Adam sitting next to her, Amanda was fairly certain the other woman would have no trouble snuggling. She instantly chastised herself for the malicious thought. Despite her obvious attempts to gain Adam's attention, Rose had surprised her with her fortitude.

"Well, I can s-s-say we never have anything even-r-r-remotely like this in England," Evan added, his irritation clearly evident.

The marshal squinted one eye as he studied the younger man. "So, what brings you to America?" he asked, and Amanda sensed a lawman's interest behind the question.

Being huddled on the floor between all of their bodies, the marshal and Jake seemed to be less affected by the cold, despite the freezing temperatures.

Evan shifted nervously, sharing an anxious look with his sister. She shook her head ever so slightly. Evan threw Tucker a wary look. "Personal business," he told him, before once again sinking into a belabored silence.

Marshal Tucker continued to study him through slitted eyes, one eyebrow cocking upward suspiciously. "Mmm-hmm."

Color flooded Evan's face, not unlike her own when she had something to hide.

Amanda caught Mr. Bass's hostile glare resting on the brother and sister before he realized he had an audience. His face quickly settled into its normal serene expression and he smiled at Amanda. She hesitantly returned his smile, again wondering at the man's story in regards to the two Brits, especially since from the very beginning, they acted as though they didn't know the man.

"What about you, Preacher Girl? Where's your *Good Lord* now?"

Amanda was more startled that Jake had spoken than by the name he called her. She could count on one hand the number of words he had vocalized since their trip began in Memphis. She felt Adam's arm tighten against her shoulder at Jake's hostile tone.

"I'm not a preacher," she disavowed hotly. Regardless of his obvious attempt to use it as an insult, she decided to take the title as a compliment. She wasn't ashamed of her Lord, nor afraid to speak out for Him. "And He's right here, Jake," she told him softly. "Listening to every word, hearing every thought."

Jake wasn't the only one who squirmed, glancing nervously around the semidark interior of the coach. "You sound just like my sister."

The statement was a mixture of frustration and reverence. Amanda was astounded at the emotion threading through his words. To hear such a cold-blooded killer speak of someone with such love brought home to Amanda the fact that no one is completely heartless. Since he had finally decided to act less antagonistic, she determined to treat him with polite courtesy despite his disparaging attitude toward her.

"Where is your sister, Jake?" She asked the question hoping to open some kind of dialogue with him.

There was a bite in his words when he answered. "None of your business."

Amanda bit down on her bottom lip to keep from snapping back at the man. She took a deep breath, rejecting the thought of counting to ten to still her temper. It had never helped her in the past.

"You say I sound like her. I take it you are saying she's a godly woman."

"For all the good it does her," he hissed. "Her Good Lord didn't keep her from being attacked by a man. A preacher man at that. So you can save your trite sayings. Not everyone appreciates them."

She heard Adam's swift intake of breath and wished now she hadn't answered Jake's initial verbal attack. Those last blistering words would in all probability bring back memories for Adam that were best forgotten. How odd that the same thing that happened to Adam's friend had happened to Jake's sister. What was the world coming to that two such men of God could do such a thing?

"What was your sister's name?" Adam asked quietly, something in his voice alerting the other man and everyone else it wasn't just a simple question.

Jake glanced at Adam, searching his face through the dim light filtering into the coach from outside. He frowned.

Tucked into Adam's side as she was, she could feel his breathing quicken as he stared back at Jake. They studied each other in complete silence, the tension in the stage mounting while the others looked on in confusion. Some secret communication passed between them that only they understood.

Suddenly, Jake's haughty posture collapsed, his brow

folding inward. "Lillie. Her name was Lillie." He watched Adam carefully, as though he expected the name to mean something to him.

And at that moment, like a bolt out of the blue, Amanda knew. Jake's sister and Adam's friend were one and the same. Her eyes widened as she whirled on Jake.

"You were the one who killed the preacher!" she burst out.

Jake turned to her in surprise. "What do you know about it?"

Before she could answer, Adam interrupted with quiet conviction. "I understand now. I couldn't figure out where I had seen you before." His voice turned whisper soft. "You look like her."

Jake turned his attention back to Adam. His eyes glistened with suppressed animosity. "So, you're the one she told me about. She never mentioned your name, but I got the impression you were the closest thing to Sir Galahad that anyone could ever hope to meet."

Amanda could certainly agree with *that* assessment, although hearing the words coming from another woman filled her stomach with that queasy kind of jealousy she had experienced earlier. She felt Adam shift uneasily at the backhanded compliment.

"I'm sorry I wasn't there to protect her," he told Jake quietly, the pain of failure evident in his voice.

Several heartbeats went by before Jake practically growled, "Doesn't matter. I took care of the problem."

"And if you weren't already going to hang for that murder in San Francisco, you'd be swinging from a rope for that, too," Marshal Tucker interrupted their tense exchange.

Jake met the marshal's severe glare with one of his own. "Yeah, and I'd do it again." He then retreated once again into silence, pulling on his armor of isolation and ignoring everybody.

"You're the reason I'm out of jail, aren't you?" Adam stated, bringing Jake's reluctant attention back to him once again.

Jake stared at Adam a long time before he finally answered. His face switched from defiant to regret. "I didn't know you went to prison. I guess you can thank Preacher Lady's Good Lord you didn't hang."

"Will you stop calling me that?" Amanda snapped.

Both men ignored her.

"They didn't have enough evidence to hang me, so they just sent me to prison. At least the *good* people of Indian Wells had enough scruples not to hang a man without evidence, even though they had no problem condemning him for something he didn't do."

Adam didn't make the word *good* sound like a compliment. He studied Jake curiously. "What made you confess?"

Jake buried his face in the quilt he was struggling to keep wrapped around him with one hand since the other was manacled to the marshal. It seemed as though he wasn't going to answer, but then he sighed. "Lillie told me she would never speak to me again if I didn't."

Adam quickly sat forward, dislodging the quilt wrapped around him and Amanda. Adam seemed impervious to the below-freezing temperatures that instantly engulfed them. "You've seen Lillie? Is she…is she all right?"

There was such intense excitement in his voice that Amanda became convinced the feelings he had for the woman were stronger than even he believed. She felt as though tiny shards of ice were being slowly imbedded into her heart.

"She was," Jake answered. "I don't know, now. When I refused to admit to the preacher's killing, she told me she would never speak to me again. The next day, she disappeared. I tried to find her, but it's like she's a phantom. So I wrote the letter admitting my guilt. I thought if she learned you were out of prison, she would contact me again." His voice became husky. "I want to tell her I'm sorry before I die."

A sympathetic silence filled the coach at his impassioned words. Amanda never expected to feel compassion for such a murderer, but she did. No one who spoke with such love and concern could be completely without heart.

Amanda couldn't let the matter rest as it was. "Jake," she tried. "Lillie was trying to remind you that vengeance belongs to God. The Good Book says that He will repay our wrongs."

His lips curled into a sneer, and she caught her breath when he leaned toward her, his eyes gleaming with malice in the semidarkness. Adam swiftly moved, his eyes flashing a warning that Jake was quick to heed. He hastily sat back, retreating to a safe distance.

"Our mama taught us God expects us to be his hands and feet," Jake told her, keeping a guarded eye on Adam. "That's what I did. I allowed *my* hands to be His instrument of justice."

How could a man who had such a mother and sister have gone so wrong?

"And do you also allow them to be His instruments of love and compassion?"

His eyes flickered briefly before he tucked his head farther into the quilt and ignored her question. "And you wonder why I call you Preacher Girl."

Amanda didn't know where to take the conversation from here. She hadn't meant to sound preachy, but she was compelled to remind the man of his obviously godly upbringing. Surely, something of that man was left inside that empty shell.

"You say you don't know where Lillie is?" Adam asked.

He hesitantly met Adam's questioning look. "No, but I

know she's safe. She told me you talked her out of killing herself. You should know she regrets that she lost hope and had those thoughts. She's thankful for your guidance at that time." He paused for a heartbeat. "And so am I."

"Thank God she's alive," Adam said. "When she disappeared, I was afraid."

Jake tugged the quilt tighter. "I owe you," he finished quietly.

Adam shook his head. "No. You owe me nothing. You paid that debt when you confessed to the killing and I was released from prison."

"I owe you for the two years you spent there on my behalf."

Jake once again withdrew into a concluding silence.

Amanda looked from one man to the other. She didn't believe in coincidence. The Good Lord had brought these two together to bring healing to their hearts. The haunted look was gone from Adam's eyes and the dark void of Jake's was now filled with something less menacing.

The entire coach settled into silence once more, broken only by the wailing of the wind outside. Despite the bone-chilling temperatures, or maybe because of them, Amanda found herself drifting off to sleep.

Adam tried to carefully move out from under Amanda so as not to awaken her, but her eyes flitted open, blinking up at him in drowsy unawareness.

"Stay put. I need to check on the mules."

She sat bolt upright, blinking in the harsh light coming in from the door that Sam had just exited.

"It's stopped snowing?" she asked.

Adam nodded, tucking the quilt tightly about her.

Stepping over the marshal and his prisoner, Adam swung himself out the door into a cold, white world.

He followed the deep ruts of Sam's footprints to the

front of the wagon. Sam was brushing snow off the tarps he had used to cover the mules. When he had removed enough snow, he flipped the tarps off to uncover the beasts.

To Adam's amazement, the mules had survived the harsh storm even though they were buried up to their bellies in soft, white powder. Their braying suddenly invaded the peaceful quiet of the storm-swept prairie around them.

Sam grinned. "Somebody wants his breakfast."

Adam surveyed the area. It was obvious which direction the wind had gusted from: snow buried one side of the coach nearly to the top of the canvas roof. The coach's other side was fairly free, with snow covering only half the wheels. In the distance, the snow had been stopped in its raging pursuit by scrub and mesquite bushes, making little hills all over the surrounding plain. From the intensity of the storm, Adam was surprised the land was covered by only about two feet of snow.

He was aware of Amanda's presence before she spoke. "How bad is it?"

It was Sam who answered. "Not bad at all. We need to unbury the coach. Then we can be on our way."

Adam squinted at the sun shining brightly in the eastern sky. "Looks to be about ten o'clock."

Amanda pulled out her pocket watch and flipped it open. She grinned at Adam, and he felt the force of her pansy-colored eyes all the way to his freezing toes.

"Ten minutes to," she told him.

"Let's get everyone out of the wagon and clear the snow from it so we can get going," Sam said. He plowed through the drifts back to the stage door and bellowed, "Everyone out! We need everyone's help if we're going to get out of here quickly."

Evan stepped out carefully, trying to place his footsteps in the tracks the others had left. "Surely not the women," he protested.

Amanda frowned at him. "I can help."

"So can I," Rose told him as she peered from the stage door at the vast panorama of white.

Evan opened his mouth to protest, but his sister silenced him with a look. Pressing his lips tightly together, he reached to assist her from the stage. Adam had to give her credit for being willing to pitch in. He was fairly certain such things were beneath her where she came from.

The others were already using their hands as shovels to remove as much of the piled snow as possible from around the sides of the coach and the wheels. Adam joined them, as did the Nightingtons. The marshal and his prisoner were using their unmanacled hands to shove snow away from the partially buried mules.

With everyone helping, it didn't take long before the stage was free enough to continue the journey. Everyone piled back into the coach, much wetter and colder than before. Adam insisted Amanda ride inside, as well. The storm had left behind a bone-chilling cold and he didn't want Amanda out in it.

The mulish look on her face told him she was about to object, but he reminded her he was the conductor for this leg of the journey. She glared at him in impotent rage, which only amused him.

With a huff of protest, she clambered inside.

Adam joined Sam on the driver's seat. "This snow is really going to slow us down," he pointed out.

Sam, ever the optimist, disagreed. "Naw. Them mules is hungry. Just sit back and watch 'em go."

Adam decided to trust the frontiersman's knowledge of the ornery animals and did just that.

At one snap of the whip, the mules plowed forward through the snow at a fairly steady pace. They were intent on reaching shelter and the food it promised, and their angry braying reverberated throughout the silent prairie as they plodded along as quickly as their buried legs would allow them.

After about twenty miles, the snow began to thin until, the farther they traveled, it became patchy and sparse, allowing them to once again pick up speed.

They reached the next station and exchanged the tired mules for fresh ones, had a measly breakfast of bread and coffee, and were on their way once again.

They traveled mile after mile over flat prairie, stopping and exchanging mules along the way. At times, Amanda rode outside on top and Adam sat inside, but he much preferred sitting on top with Amanda than having to put up with Rose's constant bids for attention.

They passed the Phantom Hill station without stopping as there were no mules to spare in this isolated place as of yet. The burned-out fort buildings were eerie shadows against the backdrop of a waning moon.

Although most of the buildings of the fort had been burned down when the soldiers had left it years before, the stone structures were in good enough shape to be used by the Butterfield as a station house and corral. An eighty-foot-deep well provided water, and a man named Burlington and his wife made it their home.

They were heavily into Apache territory now, and Adam rode in tense silence for mile after mile while Amanda and the new driver, Emmett, argued back and forth about the merits of the landscape, the stations and whether the Butterfield was fulfilling its promise to open up the country.

Adam was content to simply listen to Amanda's voice and feel her presence beside him. If not for the possibility of danger, he would have enjoyed this time together, getting to know the woman from the child he remembered. Each hour that passed opened his eyes to the new and remarkable woman she had become.

It amazed him that she had remained so unspoiled, and

he attributed that to her mother, who was a remarkable woman herself. He knew Mrs. Ross only wanted what was best for her daughter, but how could she not see that that same daughter was meant to be so much more than some man's chattel?

The man they wanted to marry her to was brutal. He was mean, domineering, and materialistic, and Adam would be hanged before he saw Amanda tied to such a person.

He studied her unobtrusively. She wasn't exactly pretty, but then, neither was she totally plain. How could a woman be considered plain when her face lit up with excitement and those marvelous eyes sparkled with energy? The freckles dancing across her nose and cheeks only added to the picture of an unspoiled life.

As though she could sense his appraisal, she turned and met his look with a questioning one of her own. Several seconds of unspoken communication passed between them. Her eyes darkened, her lips parted slightly, and his breathing quickened in response.

What was going through her mind that put such a strange expression on her face, an expression that tightened his stomach into a knot? He should warn her it was dangerous to look at a man like that. Before he could think of anything to say, she turned away, and he was finally able to take a breath.

Ten more days and they should reach their destination. It couldn't come too soon for him.

Chapter 13

Amanda rechecked the harnesses on the mules while Adam got something to eat. Something had passed between them several days ago, and she was still shaking from it. For just an instant, she thought he had been about to kiss her. The look in his eyes had been so intense, it both frightened and excited her.

When they got to San Francisco, she fully intended to have a long conversation with him. Whenever they were together, the very air seemed to be full of charged energy. She needed to know if he felt it, too, or if it was just her wishful imagination.

For the time being, she had to concentrate on just getting to San Francisco.

She leaned against a mule, staring at the miles of desert that stretched into the distance. At least they were out of the snow, although, according to the driver, they would probably encounter more when they reached the New Mexico Territory. It had been a bizarre year in regard to weather.

The temperatures had increased the farther west they traveled across Texas, and they had been able to make up much of the time they had lost earlier while dealing with floods, Indians and snow.

Now they were about to cross the Staked Plain, one of the savannas of America. Its true name was the Llano Estacado. A certain tradition spoke of it deriving its name from the Spaniards who had traveled through earlier staking out a road from San Antonio to Santa Fe.

Whatever its name, Amanda was not looking forward to crossing it. For seventy-five miles they would be without any water except what they could carry with them. There were no stations between here and the Pecos River. Therefore they would have to take a remuda of mules along with them to change teams on the journey. The only encouraging thought was they would be able to travel much faster on the sunbaked plain.

The passengers finally exited the tent the station agents were using as housing while they were building a proper home and made their way to the coach, climbing inside with a mixture of anticipation and dread.

"I'm riding on top with you and Emmett," Amanda told Adam in a tone of voice that warned him she would brook no refusal. He stared solemnly at her for several seconds before jerking his head in a nod of acceptance and holding out his hand to help her up.

The temperatures were warm enough during the day that she was able to discard her jacket and take advantage of the cool breezes blowing across the prairie. She couldn't wait to get to San Francisco so she could finally have a real bath. The few times they were able to dip in the rivers and creeks just weren't adequate enough.

They let the mules fill up with water at Mustang Springs, hoping to use the stored canteens sparingly during the seventy-five-mile trip across the desert.

The flat view spread out before them, heavily scattered scrub resembling black dots on a sable background. Emmett told her they were mesquite bushes, but they were now traveling along at such a clip all she could see was a blur.

The plant that most caught her attention was the Spanish dagger. It certainly lived up to its name, its long, tapered and sharp-pointed leaves a good representation of the lethal weapon.

All along the way, they passed decaying animal carcasses. The sunbaked plain stretched far into the distance, a barren wasteland that gave Amanda shivers. That was pretty much how she had seen her life for the past several years: barren and unproductive. Yet, even here, signs of life abounded, stirred into existence by a recent rain.

Much as she had been stirred to life again by finding Adam. What her parents had considered merely a childish infatuation had in truth been a bonding of souls. At least on her part. It all made sense to her now.

A large herd of antelope charged away at their approach, skipping and hopping gracefully across the hard-baked sand. Birds called to each other, relieving the silence that was otherwise broken only by the pounding of the coach as it passed.

Periodically, the coach would lunge as they hit a mound of dirt piled high by tunneling prairie dogs. When she nearly flew from the seat for the third time, Adam tucked her next to his side and kept a firm arm around her. She happily settled into his embrace, despite what his nearness did to her composure. They were nearing the end of their journey, and she wanted to take every opportunity to spend as much time with him as possible. She had an ominous feeling that when their trip ended, Adam would disappear from her life again.

They stopped several times to change mules with those in the remuda. Each stop took more time, as the mules were still unbroken and balked at being put into the harness. Eventually, they would be on their way again, but not before exhausting the driver and the men herding the extra mules. It was a comical sight watching their antics, but she doubted it was appreciated by the men themselves.

Day gave way to night, and the Spanish dagger plants resembled men rising up from the desert floor. Being in Apache territory, Amanda found herself quickly reaching for her gun over and over again.

Emmett spit a wad of tobacco juice over the side before glancing her way. "Bit nervous, are ya?"

"We were attacked by a Comanche raiding party a while back," Adam stated.

Understanding filled Emmett's face. "Well, the Apache have been quiet lately. I don't think we'll have a problem."

Amanda certainly hoped his prediction came true.

They traveled on in silence for some time before Adam said, "You should get some sleep."

Amanda had her doubts about being able to sleep with the excitement of having Adam holding her so close. She was filled with a warm peace in just knowing that, as well as her Lord, Adam was there to watch over her. To her surprise, her body reacted to the feeling by relaxing until her eyelids drooped.

Sleep came, and with it dreams of a home and children; little boys with mischievous hazel eyes and little girls with large pansy eyes who, unlike their mother, were quite beautiful.

Adam stared at the sleeping woman in his arms and wondered what dreams were putting that beatific smile on her face. If not for Emmett's curious gaze, Adam would have kissed Amanda's perky little face.

Emmett cocked one eyebrow at him. "Boy, you got it bad, ain't ya?"

Adam didn't bother to deny it. What was the use? Truth be told, without Amanda, he was only half-alive. She had always been the driving force behind him. Without her, he had wandered from place to place, never able to settle down.

With her, settling down was all he recently thought about. He had rebelled against his father's desire to mold him into his own image of the great southern banker. Now, that didn't seem quite so bad. He had always loved the challenge of working with money, and he had a head for figures. It was the marrying part he had balked at.

There were definitely worse things than spending a day at the bank and then coming home to a loving wife and children. But only if that woman was Amanda.

He had finally realized it wasn't the thought of marrying that had bothered him; it was the thought of doing so with someone other than Amanda. She had been too young to even think about a romantic notion when he had left. Now he realized that God had been guiding him all along.

Amanda needed time to grow up and experience life on her own without him there to interfere. But where did they go from here?

Darkness gave way to dawn, and Amanda slowly awakened in his arms. She peered up at him in the increasing light, a slow smile forming on her face that just about turned him inside out.

Realization of their circumstances brought a swift change, and she sat up abruptly, moving out of his embrace. Embarrassed color flooded her face and he cocked a brow, a slow smile turning up his lips. He would give a month's wages to know what dreams had inspired such discomfiture.

"Where are we?" she asked as she rubbed the sleep from her eyes.

Emmett answered, "We're coming up on the Pecos River."

Adam could see the Guadalupe Mountains in the distance rising majestically against the clear morning sky. He breathed a sigh of relief. They would stop at Pope's Camp long enough to get something to eat and possibly wash up a little. They were so far behind schedule they couldn't afford to waste too much time here, but it would be a good idea if everyone had a chance to stretch a little. He blew the horn to give those at the station forewarning of their approach.

When the coach came to a stop in front of the adobe building, Amanda lifted the mail pouch from between her feet. Keeping the mail with them would allow them both to eat and save a little time. It was a smart move on her part, and his look assured her of such. Soft color once again pinkened her cheeks at his approval.

Breakfast wasn't much, but at least it was filling. He took advantage of the shortcake, coffee and dried beef, but declined the raw onion. The two Brits had wrinkled their noses at the mean fare, but hunger drove them to consume it anyway. Even Mr. Bass had scarfed down a second helping.

Adam had just poured himself a second cup of coffee at the stove when the door opened and three men walked in. His instincts went on high alert without apparent reason except that three men coming out of nowhere in the middle of nowhere was a mite unusual.

The first thing that stood out about them was their great need for a bath. Their strong body odor preceded them as they walked across the room. The second thing of note was each man sported a sidearm and rifle, not unusual in this area of the country, but unsettling to Adam's nerves nonetheless. He watched as their glances swiftly circumnavigated the room and its occupants.

"Is this here where we can catch the stage to San Francisco?" the seeming leader of the pack asked. The cold, lifeless eyes turning his way had Adam reaching for his gun, but another voice stopped his hand inches from his holster.

"I wouldn't do that if I was you, mister."

The three men had spread out in different directions, and Adam had missed the one who now stood at his back. He sighed soundlessly. After everything they had been through, they were now about to be robbed of the mail.

His first thought was that he couldn't let it happen. Glancing about the room at the passengers in their various states of alarm, any thoughts of being a hero were quickly squashed. He couldn't take the chance on anyone getting hurt.

The barrel of a gun prodded him from behind. "Hands in the air, nice and easy like."

He complied, and the man carefully pulled his Colts from his holsters. He caught Amanda's furious eyes and frowned a warning. He wouldn't put it past her to take on all three men and get herself killed in the process. The thought made his blood turn to ice.

Her nostrils flared outward as she fought her instinctive desire to do something.

"There's no money on this stage," Amanda told them. "You're wasting your time."

"Did I ask you, boy?"

Adam threw her another warning look, and she subsided, the gun pointing at his back an effective deterrent.

The leader strode across to where the marshal and Jake were seated at the table. Adam tensed as the man pointed his gun at the lawman.

"Now, Marshal, how 'bout you take out the key and unhandcuff my friend here."

All eyes focused on the trio.

So that was what this was all about. Jake's gang was here to rescue him. Adam had no idea how they had gotten the information that Jake would be on this stage, but they had obviously been hanging around here for some time since they couldn't have known the stage would arrive today as they were several days behind schedule.

Marshal Tucker looked as if he was about to object, but a cocking of the hammer pointed at his head quickly put the idea out of his mind. He slowly withdrew the key from his pocket and unlocked the manacles.

Jake rubbed his freed wrist and stared at the marshal in glacial silence. He took the key from the marshal's hand and snapped the recently released manacle onto the chair back, locking it firmly in place, then snapped the other end back on the marshal. He grinned as he tauntingly held up the key.

"I'll just take this along with me."

"You want I should kill him?" the other man asked.

"No!"

At Amanda's shocked scream, the other man whirled, his gun aimed at her heart. Reacting instinctively, Adam went for his missing gun only to be slammed in the head from behind. He struggled against the encroaching darkness, his mind fighting his body in order to protect Amanda. As from a distance, a shot rang out and Adam's only thought as he tumbled into unconsciousness was that without Amanda, he had no reason to live.

Jake knocked the man's hand and the bullet went wild, imbedding itself into the wall behind Amanda's head.

Rose screamed, burying her head against her brother's chest. All color had drained from Evan's face and he looked as if he was on the verge of collapsing. Mr. Bass was the only seemingly cool one among them. He stood resolutely, not even looking at the men, but Amanda got the distinct impression he had catalogued every detail about them.

"What the…?" The other man spun around, glaring at Jake. "What's the big idea?"

"She was unarmed, Bob."

Bob's eyes went wide and then he squinted at Amanda. *"She?"*

"Never mind," Jake told him, quickly relieving the others of their weapons. "Just turn the mules loose and let's get out of here."

Adam's unconscious form lying on the floor sent a surge of fear and rage flooding through Amanda. She fixed her eyes on the man who had clubbed him, and her fingers flexed near her empty holster. All of the admonishments she had given Jake about vengeance belonging to the Lord flew from her mind. For the first time, she could actually empathize with his position.

"So help me, if you've killed Adam, I will track you down if it takes the rest of my life."

Jake glanced at her as he bent to Adam's prostrate form. He put two fingers against the pulse in Adam's neck, and then one side of his mouth cocked upward. "Don't worry, Preacher Girl. He's fine. He's just going to have one doozy of a headache for a while."

Amanda quickly crossed the room and dropped to Adam's side. Blood oozed from a gash on the back of his head. She glared at Jake, and he grinned, holding his palms up.

"It wasn't me."

The third man had moved closer to Rose, the lust in his eyes clearly evident even from a distance. Amanda's stomach churned as his gaze slowly slid over the other woman's body.

"Hey, Jake. Can we take this one with us?"

Jake stood, brushing his hands against his dirty denims. He studied Rose as thoroughly as his partner, an avaricious gleam filling his eyes. It was obvious from their appearance that the Brits had money. A slow smile indicated he thought the idea of taking her along was worth pursuing.

"Over my dead body," Evan snarled, pushing his sister behind him. Amanda had to give him credit for daring courage, if not for his poor choice of words.

"That could be arranged," the other man growled, thumping Evan in the chest with his pistol.

Everything inside Amanda urged her to try something to defuse the situation despite the overwhelming odds. "Just remember, Jake," Amanda warned him, "she's someone's sister, too."

The reminder had the desired effect. The smile disappeared from Jake's face. He swallowed hard, his jaw working back and forth. He turned to Marshal Tucker, his rage at being thwarted focusing on the lawman.

"You've hounded me for over a year, but you won't do so again."

He picked up Adam's gun and aimed it at the marshal, slowly cocking back the hammer. Amanda quickly rose to her feet and placed a restraining hand on his arm.

"You told Adam you owed him. I don't think he would want you to kill the marshal or anyone else." And just in case that wasn't enough deterrent, she laid her aces on the table. "Neither would Lillie."

She could hear the grinding of his teeth as he fought with whatever impulses were trying to take over his thoughts. Several tense seconds passed before he finally uncocked the hammer and slowly pointed the gun at the ceiling.

"You ain't gonna let him live, are ya?" Sam objected. "He'll be after us in no time!"

Jake continued to stare coldly at the marshal. "We'll be in Mexico before he can even find a way out of here."

The man who had gone outside to free the mules returned. "I run the mules off," he said, glancing curiously from Sam to Jake.

Jake slid the pistol into the waistband of his pants and picked up a rifle.

"Then let's get outta here."

He stopped in front of Amanda, staring at her for several long seconds. She tipped up her chin defiantly as she glared back at him.

He jerked the hat off her head and her hair surged down her back in a wavy brown mass. He took her by the chin, and she watched his lips curl slowly into a smile.

"You know, you ain't half bad to look at under all that getup," he told her. If he hadn't been holding her chin, it would have dropped at the strange comment.

He released her and picked up his hat from the table. Settling it onto his head, he grinned.

"Maybe we'll meet again, Preacher Girl."

With that, he exited the building with his companions.

Amanda once again dropped to Adam's side. Rolling him onto his back, she brushed his dark hair from his forehead.

"Get me some water!" she commanded, and Mr. Bass hurried to obey.

Chapter 14

They had to wait for the next stage coming from California before being able to travel onward. Without mules to spare, the Saint Louis–bound coach was forced to travel on with its own tired steeds and get word to the next station agent to bring some mules back to them.

It was hours before they were able to head out, minus Marshal Tucker, who confiscated an extra mule and took off after Jake and the others.

Adam wished him luck. His head still pounded, and he tugged on the bandage that was wound tightly around his wound to stem the flow of blood. Amanda cut her eyes his way, frowning.

"Leave it, Adam."

He grinned at her bossy tone, relieved the horror of what had happened had finally disappeared from her eyes. She was hovering over him like a mother hen. He would appreciate her concern and closeness if he wasn't so irritated with his own weakness. It had been hours before his legs had felt anything less than pudding.

When he had finally struggled back from dark unconsciousness, he had opened his eyes to worried violet ones staring anxiously down at him. He couldn't even begin to describe the feeling that had rolled through him. She was alive. His first thought had been, *Thank You, God*!

He had grabbed her, pulling her down to his chest and burying his face in her cascading tresses. He held her so tightly, she eventually gave a protesting squeak and he reluctantly loosened his hold. She had taken it from there, treating him like some kind of invalid.

In the past few hours, he had determined two things. One, this was no kind of life for Amanda, and two, if it was no life for Amanda, then it was certainly no life for him because he didn't want to spend another day of *his* life without her.

The rest of the journey seemed almost anticlimactic after all they had been through. They encountered no other major problems, and the minor ones, such as balking mules and blowing dust, were easily overcome.

He was anxious traveling through Apache territory without weapons, but they rode on with no trouble. He felt certain it had more to do with Amanda's Good Lord than anything else. Someone else might have focused on the negatives of what had happened to them on this journey; he was more focused on the positive aspects of how God had kept them safe despite all they had experienced.

He noticed Amanda trying to observe him surreptitiously to make certain he was all right after his clubbing, but any time she glanced his way, every nerve in his body stood to attention. He would meet her look, and his thoughts and feelings must have been reflected in his eyes, because color would fill her cheeks, and she would quickly turn away.

The awareness between them grew daily until it was all he could do to keep from telling her of his feelings. But, he had a job to do first, and a bouncing stage was no place to declare himself. When he did so, he wanted to be able to look into her eyes and see her reaction.

After reaching Tucson in Arizona Territory, they increased the number of stock from four stubborn mules to six well-trained horses, and their speed increased. Mr. Hall, who had been hired to stock the stage line from Tucson to Los Angeles, had procured some of the finest teams available, and he drove the route with the confidence of a man familiar with the terrain.

Amanda took an instant liking to the rather gruff man and, for once, she was treated with the polite courtesy of a gentleman for a lady. Regardless of what she might say otherwise, Adam could tell it meant a lot to her.

They reached Fort Yuma and braced themselves for the next round of dry desert terrain. Adam, tired of eating sandy grit, turned his thoughts to the green fields of Tennessee.

His time in prison had given him a greater appreciation of his home. It was why he had chosen to live there and drive the first sixty miles of the Butterfield Overland Mail. It was as close as he had dared to get to Amanda before he could figure out why his thoughts turned to her so often. Needless to say, he had been unprepared for the flood of emotions seeing her again had caused.

Just below Yuma, they reached the California line. The road passed through fertile valleys full of cattle and agricultural fields. Mile after mile, they passed prosperous ranches of the wealthy, as well as little adobe houses of the less fortunate.

Amanda turned to him, her look one of surprise. "I had no idea," she said softly.

Neither had he. His ideas of the western part of the country were being quickly revised. It was a lot more settled than he had at first imagined. He was about to make a comment and then stopped short at the enticing picture she made.

She had taken to wearing her hair down, and it hung to her waist, the sun turning it from dark brown into a molten copper. She had propped a hat on her head and her petite figure was encased in close-fitting buckskin pants, but she exuded an aura of femininity that he knew was a result of her privileged upbringing among some of the South's finest families.

The beauty of the surrounding landscape made her eyes shine with appreciation, or perhaps it was his company that did so. He would certainly like to think that was the case.

He swallowed hard and turned away before his thoughts could start wandering into forbidden territory again.

When the terrain became dangerous Adam insisted Amanda ride inside with the others. He needed to stay focused, and her nearness had grown more disturbing with each passing mile.

Amanda sat beside Mr. Bass, silently fuming. At the rate they were going, it wouldn't be long before they reached San Francisco. The end of their journey and the return trip to face her parents was looming like an overwhelming specter.

Her uneasy thoughts were brought to an abrupt halt when Rose said something to her. Amanda glanced at her apologetically. "I'm sorry. What did you say?"

Rose smiled, and it was the friendliest smile Amanda had ever received from her. "I asked you what Tennessee was like."

Amanda readily told her about Uncle Taylor and her life growing up in Tennessee. Talking about it made her suddenly homesick, and her parents' smothering love no longer seemed so odious. She missed her mother's warm embraces, her father's smiles. Would they welcome her back after this recent escapade? The more pressing question was, would Adam return home with her? The thought of going back without him simply held no appeal.

Rose embarked on a tale of her life in Britain and how they came to be in the United States. It seemed to Amanda as though Mr. Bass's interest perked up when Rose spoke, though he gave no outward sign of it other than a slight tensing of his body. He was always careful not to look at the couple, which was curious in itself. She wondered if she would ever know the story behind these three.

When they reached the next station, they traded horses and wagon. The time and distance was quickly passing now, as the roads from Tucson through California had been traversed for several years. They crossed through the mountains at the Pacheco Pass and drew closer to the coast, which put them now one hundred and sixty-three miles from San Francisco.

The terrain became more treacherous as they traveled through craggy hills and ravines, many whose bottoms could not be seen from their perspective high above them.

When they reached San Jose, they happily switched back to the Concord coach, thankful for the comfort on their last leg of the journey.

Since the roads were now less hazardous, Amanda returned to her position beside Adam on top of the stage and shared the exhilaration of the amazing scenery passing mile after mile. They traveled from desert to mountains to valleys filled with miles of produce.

The sun was just appearing in the eastern sky as they topped the rise leading into San Francisco. The sprawling settlement stretched out before them, the bay glistening in the distance. Amanda caught her breath at the immense expanse of water.

Before long, they reached the pavement of the city, and their pace quickened. They flew up and down the city streets, passing openmouthed pedestrians until they at last arrived in front of the Plaza Hotel where the Butterfield Overland Mail office adjoined it on one side. The driver pulled the horses to a stop.

He handed Adam the reins and climbed down to open the door and help Rose from the coach, with Evan and Mr. Bass following close behind. Rose looked up at the Plaza Hotel and sighed.

"I have never been so glad to see a hotel in my life!"

Neither Evan nor Mr. Bass said anything, but their weariness was just as evident as they pulled their luggage from under the seats. After twenty-five days on the road, the sudden release of stress left them all sagging. Despite the hurdles they had overcome, they were still on time according to the contract. That the other stages had been managing the crossing in twenty-one days Amanda simply chose to ignore, merely thankful they had arrived on time and relatively unscathed.

Amanda had to concur with Rose's comment on the hotel, but she was too busy to take further notice of the passengers as they disappeared inside. She was occupied with writing their arrival time in the logbook while Adam jumped down and removed packages to take to the post office.

Amanda signed off the passengers and headed for the Butterfield office. She handed the agent a letter that Mr. Dailey had requested she give him when they arrived. He read it quickly, glancing up at her with a peculiar look.

Adam joined her in the office and handed the agent the mailbag.

"You are Mr. Clark?"

Adam acknowledged him with a nod.

"And this is *Miss* Ross?" he asked, his curious inspection of her making her decidedly uneasy.

Again Adam acknowledged him with a nod, but this

time it was followed by a look warning the agent to be careful of what he said. Amanda sighed inwardly. Adam was being his same overprotective self, as though she were a child who needed defending.

The wary look on the other man's face assured Amanda he had gotten the nonverbal message. He cleared his throat.

"Well, Miss Ross, there will be no return engagement of your services. The Butterfield appreciates your willingness to step in and chaperone Miss Nightington, but when you return you will have to do so as a passenger. We will, of course, fulfill your return fare."

"I can assure you, sir," she told him firmly, without refuting his statement of her being a chaperone, "I had no other intention."

Glancing at Adam, he cleared his throat again. "Good. Good. Well, let's get on with it, then."

Amanda relinquished the logbook with a profound sense of relief. She and Adam apprised him of the difficulties they had had along the way. His eyes widened with each narrative, his look changing from haughty to respect mingled with doubt.

She and Adam took their leave of him after arranging for a return fare. The stage was so booked up, it would be a week before they could make the return trip. It would seem that word of the stage line had spread and many people wanted to return to the East Coast. Even after all they went through, she, like most people, would still prefer it to an ocean voyage, which would make it necessary to travel through the Cape of Good Hope, the graveyard of the Pacific.

Adam took her arm. "Let's book rooms at the Plaza, and then we need to find somewhere private to talk."

It was the very thing she longed to do, yet she was suddenly afraid. She had faced Indians, storms and murderers with less trepidation than she was feeling right now.

"All right."

They dodged moving traffic as they crossed the busy street, and only Adam's guidance kept her from getting run over as she gawked at the teeming city. She wasn't sure what she had expected, but it certainly wasn't this.

Adam procured them rooms and then followed her to hers, leaning against the wall by her door.

"I ordered a bath for you," he said, grinning. "I knew it would be one of the first things you would want to do."

She smiled her grateful appreciation. Reaching up, she trailed her fingers across the short beard he hadn't taken time to shave off since their journey began.

He sucked in a sharp breath at her touch, his smile turning wry. "I am headed for the barber's down the street," he told her, his husky voice sending little tingles all over her body. "After I remove some of this facial hair, I intend to take a bath, as well. How about if I meet you back here at—" he pulled his pocket watch out and glanced at it "—at noon? We'll get some lunch."

"That would be fine," she agreed, not really wanting him to leave. But there was something she needed to do as well before they had their talk. It was time Adam saw her as the woman she was and not the child she had been.

Their eyes met once again, and her breathing faltered at the look in his eyes.

Adam took the key from her shaking fingers and pushed open the door. "I'll wait until you're inside," he said softly.

Not really aware of what she was doing, she entered the room and turned to look at him. She slowly closed the door and leaned her back against it, trying to still the pounding of her heart.

It was several seconds before she heard him walk away.

Taking a deep breath, she glanced about her. Although this hotel was nothing like the Gayoso with its modern conveniences, it wasn't bad for such a rough city. But she didn't have time to appreciate the hotel. She was a woman on a mission, and that mission was to impress Adam with how much she had matured in the past few years.

She slipped some of her gold coins from the bag she always carried hidden in her jacket and dropped them into the secret pocket she had sewn inside. She then placed the bag under the bed's mattress and hurried out to find a dress that would make Adam sit up and take notice.

She found what she was looking for in a little dress shop not far from the hotel. She chose a princess-style dress that was cut in one piece without a waistline, the molded bodice and less flared bell skirt more flattering than those of past years. The yellow sprigged muslin dress over a new crinoline petticoat belling out from behind would make her tiny waist look even tinier. The old-fashioned and layered garments of the past that had caused her such irritation now, in the more modern styles, gave her a sense of deep satisfaction. Even she could see the change it made to her appearance.

The color of the dress turned her flowing hair from a drab brown to a glowing chestnut and intensified the near-plum color of her eyes. She gave a happy little sigh, anticipating Adam's surprise and, she hoped, pleasure.

Before leaving the shop, she chose several more garments and a pair of high-button, white kid shoes to complete her new wardrobe, hoping it wouldn't be too cumbersome for their return trip. She paused as she realized she was staking an awful lot on a bunch of new clothes. Her entire life she had disparaged the conventions of the time where dress was concerned. So what had suddenly changed?

Shrugging off such thoughts, she returned to her room and enjoyed the luxury of the prepared bath in the copper tub the hotel provided. Submerging her head, she used the lavender-scented soap to wash out the dirt and grime of over two thousand miles. The water grew tepid before she was willing to leave its soothing luxury, but when she finally emerged from the tub, she felt like a new woman.

Unlike at the Gayoso, the rooms here had no electric clocks, nor clocks of any sort for that matter. She checked her pocket watch and realized that time was rapidly slipping away. Adam would be here in less than an hour, and she still needed to dress.

Adam paused outside Amanda's door and took a calming breath. He was about to take them to a new level in their relationship, but he still wasn't certain that Amanda was ready for it. Would he be ruining a friendship that had lasted a lifetime?

He straightened the jacket of the new suit he had purchased and tugged at the high collar of his shirt. Pressing his lips tightly together, he took his courage in hand and firmly rapped on the door.

It opened and for a moment he thought he had knocked on the wrong door. He was about to excuse himself when his attention was caught by glowing violet eyes. No one else had eyes like that! Amanda's mouth slowly opened into a perfect O as she stared back at him, and his did likewise as his eyes tried to reconcile with his brain the sight he was seeing.

A different Amanda stood before him, one he had never seen before. She looked purely feminine, from the top of her glistening hair pulled back by a yellow bow to hang in ringlets down her back, to the toes of her tiny feet in kid shoes peeking from beneath the belled skirt of her dress. Frankly, she quite took his breath away.

At his continued silent perusal, her cheeks pinkened with color and her eyes filled with uncertainty.

He slowly released the breath he didn't know he had been holding.

"Amanda, you look beautiful," he told her, his voice deepening with suppressed emotions. She cast her eyes to the ground, the color in her face darkening.

"You've never called me that before," she answered softly.

"Beautiful?" he asked, his brain not quite following the conversation.

"No," she told him, lifting her eyes to meet his. "Amanda."

There was a question in those plum-color depths, but at the moment, he couldn't for the life of him figure out what it was. He was still trying to figure out what had happened to his little Manny.

"Do you like me better this way?" she asked, and he couldn't miss the uncertainty in her voice.

What a heel he was. He had picked up on her little insecurities from the moment she had walked back into his life. How could he not have seen where this was leading?

He tugged her into his arms and held her close, which at the moment did nothing toward clearing his thinking.

"Manny, don't you know I would love you no matter what you wear? I loved you when you were wearing diapers, for goodness' sake."

He felt her tense, and she tried to pull away, but he refused to release her.

"What? *Now* what did I say?"

She tilted her head back, and his heart almost stopped when he saw the tears sparkling on her lashes. He cupped her face with his palms.

"Honey, what is it? What did I do?"

She stared mutely up at him, her bottom lip quivering ever so slightly, and he did the only thing that made sense to him. He kissed her with all the longing that had been building since she had waltzed back into his life.

At first, she stood rigidly in his arms, but as his frustrations passed and his kiss gentled, she slowly melted into his embrace, her lips becoming soft and pliant.

When he finally pulled back, he thought for sure his heart was going to fly right out of his chest. He sucked in a deep breath, willing her to open her eyes so he could read what was in them.

Her lids fluttered open, and she stared up at him with a dazed expression, which he thought must pretty much match his own. She placed shaking fingers against her lips and pulled in a lungful of air.

"That kiss didn't feel very brotherly."

He couldn't quite make out the tone of her voice. Pleasure? Admonishment?

"That's because I don't feel very brotherly toward you," he said huskily.

"You...you don't?"

He sighed heavily. This was the moment of truth, and he wasn't certain he was ready for it. Had he misinterpreted the signals he thought she had been sending on their trip? If he messed this up and caused her any hurt, he would never forgive himself.

Sliding a hand behind her head, he used his thumb to force her chin up until she was once again looking into his eyes. She had never been able to hide her feelings from him, and he didn't want her doing it now.

"No, Amanda, I don't. I love you like a man loves the woman he wants to marry and spend the rest of his life with."

He saw the color of her eyes deepen and suddenly fill with joy. Her lips curled up into a winsome smile. "Oh, Adam," she breathed out softly, "I hoped you would say that, because I love *you* like a woman loves the man she wants to marry and spend the rest of her life with."

He wrapped her in his arms then, closing his eyes against the force of joy flooding through him. With her head lying against his chest, she must surely feel the pounding of his heart.

"If I had my way, we would get married now and go home as man and wife...."

She pulled her head back and grinned up at him. "I'm willing."

He shook his head regretfully. "But I can't do that to your parents or mine."

Amanda's heart felt as if it grew ten times as she stared into Adam's eyes. He was such an honorable man, such a good man. How had she been so blessed?

His fingers traced a path across her cheek and over her lips. This was what she had been waiting for. For years, she had felt as if she was in some kind of limbo, but now she felt as though she was finally home.

Eyes darkened with suppressed emotion, Adam told her with a grin, "Since I doubt we will have the trouble on the return trip that we had on the way out here, you have twenty-one days to plan your wedding."

He kissed her again, and she began to fervently pray that the trip would be as uneventful as he said. As it was, it was going to be a long twenty-one days.

Epilogue

Amanda stood in front of the mirror of her bedroom back home in Tennessee and critically studied herself from every angle.

The white wedding gown was perfection. Unlike what her mother had planned for her, this dress was modestly covered in lace instead of the yards of billowing ruffles her mother had practically insisted on. Once again, she had chosen a princess style that hung straight down in the front, but belled out from behind. One day, she hoped they would do away with crinoline petticoats and tight corsets once and for all. In the meantime, she had to admit the style actually did something for her.

She smiled as she remembered Adam telling her he would marry her in buckskin if that's what she wanted. Oh, how she loved that man!

Her father entered the room and gave her a quick inspection, his eyes suddenly tearing up.

"You look beautiful."

Despite her parents' anger and frustration with her willful ways, her return to Tennessee had been met with joy, tears and forgiveness. For Adam, however, it had been a cold reunion, at least by *her* parents. Only after making them understand that with or without Adam, she would have made the trip to San Francisco, and only after hearing the stories of their encounters and how Adam had protected her, and only after realizing if she couldn't marry Adam, she wouldn't marry anyone, had her parents finally relented. They were smart people; she knew they would come around. They had been putting up with her stubborn ways for years.

"Are you ready?" her father asked.

Taking a deep breath, she nodded. Her mother handed her her wedding bouquet, straightening the bow on the back of her dress.

Taking her father's arm, she allowed him to lead her down the stairs to the entrance to their palatial ballroom. Her mother slid by her and quickly entered the room to find her seat, shutting the door behind her.

When they heard the Bridal Chorus from Wagner's opera *Lohengrin*—it had recently become a popular wedding accompaniment—Amanda straightened her shoulders. The servants opened the double doors and, from that point on, she had eyes for no one except the man waiting at the front of the room.

Adam's love had set her free. Free from self-doubts. Free from the need to conform. Free to be who God intended her to be. A woman who loved and was loved in return. Not just for who she was; not for anything she did. Adam's love was unconditional, and she had recognized that even as a child. He would give his life for her, as she would for him. It was the closest thing to God's love here on earth that any two people could hope to aspire to.

When Amanda reached his side, it was all she could

do not to throw herself into his arms. Instead, her father placed her hand in Adam's, relinquishing her into his care from this day forth.

His eyes held just a hint of what was in store for her in a lifetime as his wife. His look reached out and embraced her with a love so powerful, it left her suddenly breathless.

She listened as Adam repeated his vows in a voice firm with conviction.

He looked at her then, those incredible hazel eyes soft and shining with emotion. Although her voice wavered from reaction, she said her vows with the same certainty as he had.

When his lips finally met hers, he showed her with his kiss the promise of his eternal love.

* * * * *

REQUEST YOUR FREE BOOKS!

2 FREE INSPIRATIONAL NOVELS
PLUS 2
FREE
MYSTERY GIFTS

Love Inspired
HISTORICAL
INSPIRATIONAL HISTORICAL ROMANCE

YES! Please send me 2 FREE Love Inspired® Historical novels and my 2 FREE mystery gifts (gifts are worth about $10). After receiving them, if I don't wish to receive any more books, I can return the shipping statement marked "cancel." If I don't cancel, I will receive 4 brand-new novels every month and be billed just $4.74 per book in the U.S. or $5.24 per book in Canada. That's a savings of at least 21% off the cover price. It's quite a bargain! Shipping and handling is just 50¢ per book in the U.S. and 75¢ per book in Canada.* I understand that accepting the 2 free books and gifts places me under no obligation to buy anything. I can always return a shipment and cancel at any time. Even if I never buy another book, the two free books and gifts are mine to keep forever.

102/302 IDN F5CY

Name	(PLEASE PRINT)
Address	Apt. #
City	State/Prov. Zip/Postal Code

Signature (if under 18, a parent or guardian must sign)

Mail to the Harlequin® Reader Service:
IN U.S.A.: P.O. Box 1867, Buffalo, NY 14240-1867
IN CANADA: P.O. Box 609, Fort Erie, Ontario L2A 5X3

Want to try two free books from another series?
Call 1-800-873-8635 or visit www.ReaderService.com.

* Terms and prices subject to change without notice. Prices do not include applicable taxes. Sales tax applicable in N.Y. Canadian residents will be charged applicable taxes. Offer not valid in Quebec. This offer is limited to one order per household. Not valid for current subscribers to Love Inspired Historical books. All orders subject to credit approval. Credit or debit balances in a customer's account(s) may be offset by any other outstanding balance owed by or to the customer. Please allow 4 to 6 weeks for delivery. Offer available while quantities last.

Your Privacy—The Harlequin® Reader Service is committed to protecting your privacy. Our Privacy Policy is available online at www.ReaderService.com or upon request from the Harlequin Reader Service.

We make a portion of our mailing list available to reputable third parties that offer products we believe may interest you. If you prefer that we not exchange your name with third parties, or if you wish to clarify or modify your communication preferences, please visit us at www.ReaderService.com/consumerschoice or write to us at Harlequin Reader Service Preference Service, P.O. Box 9062, Buffalo, NY 14269. Include your complete name and address.

LIHDIR13R

ReaderService.com

Manage your account online!
- Review your order history
- Manage your payments
- Update your address

*We've designed
the Harlequin® Reader Service
website just for you.*

Enjoy all the features!
- Reader excerpts from any series
- Respond to mailings and special monthly offers
- Discover new series available to you
- Browse the Bonus Bucks catalog
- Share your feedback

Visit us at:

ReaderService.com